THE PENNILESS LORDS

In want of a wealthy wife

Meet Daniel, Gabriel, Lucien and Francis
Four lords: each down on his fortune
and each in need of a wife of means.

From such beginnings,
can these marriages of convenience turn into
something more treasured than money?

Don't miss this enthralling new quartet by
Sophia James

Read Daniel's story in
MARRIAGE MADE IN MONEY
January 2015

AUTHOR NOTE

MARRIAGE MADE IN MONEY is the first book in my new *The Penniless Lords* mini-series.

Daniel, Gabriel, Lucien and Francis are lords, down on both luck and money. With commitments to family, and great estates to support, each is forced into finding a wife of means. But the sacrificing of personal hopes and dreams does not always lead where they might imagine…and even dark clouds can sometimes have silver linings.

The first book in this series belongs to Lord Daniel Wylde, the sixth Earl of Montcliffe, newly returned from the Peninsular Wars. Is a loveless marriage of convenience to the wealthy daughter of an East London timber merchant the only way out of his substantial and mounting financial problems?

Miss Amethyst Cameron has her own conditions for their union, and she makes it known that she is as unhappy as he is with their unexpected betrothal. As a woman of trade she clearly understands that in any other circumstance the Earl of Montcliffe would never have chosen her.

MARRIAGE MADE IN MONEY

Sophia James

Published in Great Britain 2015
by Mills & Boon, an imprint of Harlequin (UK) Limited,
Eton House, 18-24 Paradise Road, Richmond, Surrey, TW9 1SR

ISBN: 978-0-263-24753-4

Harlequin (UK) Limited's policy is to use papers that are natural, renewable and recyclable products and made from wood grown in sustainable forests. The logging and manufacturing processes conform to the legal environmental regulations of the country of origin.

Printed and bound in Spain
by CPI, Barcelona

Sophia James lives in Chelsea Bay, on Auckland, New Zealand's North Shore, with her husband who is an artist. She has a degree in English and History from Auckland University and believes her love of writing was formed by reading Georgette Heyer in the holidays at her grandmother's house.

Sophia enjoys getting feedback at sophiajames.co

Previous novels by the same author:

FALLEN ANGEL
ASHBLANE'S LADY
HIGH SEAS TO HIGH SOCIETY
MASQUERADING MISTRESS
KNIGHT OF GRACE
(published as THE BORDER LORD in North America)
MISTLETOE MAGIC
(part of *Christmas Betrothals)*
ONE UNASHAMED NIGHT
ONE ILLICIT NIGHT
CHRISTMAS AT BELHAVEN CASTLE
(part of *Gift-Wrapped Governesses*)
LADY WITH THE DEVIL'S SCAR
THE DISSOLUTE DUKE
MISTRESS AT MIDNIGHT
SCARS OF BETRAYAL

Chapter One

London—June 1810

Amethyst Amelia Cameron's father loved all horses, but he especially loved his matching pair of greys.

'I doubt you will ever see others as fine, Papa, if you do indeed intend to sell them.' Amethyst tried to keep the worry from her voice as the carriage drew to a halt in the narrow lane outside number ten, Grosvenor Place. Things were changing without reason and she didn't like it.

'Well, there's the problem, my dear,' Robert Cameron replied. 'I had the best and now I want for nothing more. Take your mother, for instance. Never found another like her. Would not even have tried to.'

Amethyst smiled. Her parents' marriage had

been a love match until the day her mother had died of some undefined and quick illness, seven hours short of her thirty-second birthday. Amethyst had been all of eight and she remembered the day distinctly, the low whispers and the tears; storm clouds sweeping across the Thames.

'I do not think you should part with the pair, Papa. You can easily afford to keep them. You could afford ten times as many; every stallion and mare here in the Tattersall's sales for the next month, should you want.' Looking across the road at the generous roofs of the auction house, she wished her father might order the carriage homewards, where they could talk the matter over at their leisure.

It was not like him to decide on a course of action so quickly and she hoped he might have second thoughts and withdraw his favoured greys before the Monday sales the following week.

Yet as her father hoisted himself from the carriage his breathlessness was obvious, even such a small movement causing him difficulty. The unease Amethyst had felt over the past weeks heightened, though the sight of a man alighting from a conveyance ahead caught her attention.

After the dreadful *débâcle* of her marriage Amethyst had seldom noticed the opposite sex, shame and guilt having the effect of greying out passion. But this man was tall and big with it, the muscles beneath his superfine coat pointing to something other than the more normal indolence the *ton* seemed to excel at. He looked dangerous and untamed.

His dress marked him as an aristocrat, but his wild black hair was longer than most other men wore theirs, falling almost to his collar, the darkness highlighted by white linen. An alarming and savage beauty. She saw others turn as he walked past and wondered what it must be like to be so very visible, so awfully obvious.

'Have Elliott send the carriage back for me around two, my dear, for I am certain that will give me enough time.' Her father's words pulled her from her musing and, dragging her eyes from the stranger, she hoped Robert had not noticed her interest. 'But make sure that you have a restful time of it, too, for you have been looking tired of late.'

Shutting the door, he encouraged the conveyance on before placing his hat on his head.

His new coat was not quite fitting across his shoulders where a month ago it had been snug.

Amethyst caught her reflection in the glass as the carriage began to move. She looked older than her twenty-six years and beaten somehow. By life and by concern. Her father's actions had made her tense; after visiting his physician in London a week ago he had taken his horses straight to Tattersall's, claiming that he did not have the time for livestock he once had enjoyed.

A shock of alarm crawled up her arms and into her chest as she saw her father in conversation with the same man she had been watching. Did her father know him? What could they be speaking of? Craning her neck to see more of their engagement, she was about to turn away when the stranger looked up, his glance locking with hers across the distance.

Green. His eyes were pale green and tinged with arrogance. In shock she broke the contact, wondering about the fact that her heart was beating at twice its normal rate.

'Ridiculous,' she muttered and made certain not to look his way again. Tapping her hand hard against the roof, she was also glad when the carriage slowed to its usual speed of just above walking pace.

* * *

Lord Daniel Wylde, the sixth Earl of Montcliffe, came to Tattersall's quite regularly just to see what was on offer. Today with the sales about to begin the place was crowded.

'Ye'd be a man who knows his horseflesh, no doubt?' An older man spoke to him as they mounted the steps, no mind for introduction or proper discourse. 'My greys are up and I'd want them to go to someone who would care for their well-being.'

His accent marked him as an East-Ender, the music of the river in his words. A man made rich by the trade of goods and services, perhaps, for his coat was of fine cloth and his boots well fashioned. The well-appointed carriage he had alighted from was beginning to move away, a young woman staring back at them with concern upon her face, but Daniel's interest was snared by the mention of the greys. The superb pair he had seen yesterday belonged to this unlikely fellow? They were the entire reason he was here this morning after all, just to see who might be lucky enough to procure them.

The Repository courtyard at Tattersall's loomed, substantial pillars holding up wide verandas and housing a great number of animals and carriages.

'Your horses aren't on the block today?' Daniel could see no sign of the greys and it was more usual for those lots about to go under the hammer to be on display, especially ones so fine.

'I asked Mr Tattersall for a few days' grace just to think about things,' the other man returned, his cheeks yellowed, but his eyes sharp. 'To give me time, you understand, in case I should change my direction. The prerogative of the elderly,' he added, a wide smile showing off a set of crooked teeth.

Daniel knew he should turn and leave the man, with his roughness of speech and the impossible manners of the trading classes, but something made him stay. The sort of desperation that one perceives in the eyes of a person battling the odds, he was to think later, when all the cards had been stacked up into one long, straight and improbable line. But back then he did not have the facts of the stranger's most singular purpose.

'My name is Mr Robert Cameron. Timber merchant.' No shame or hesitation in the introduction.

'Daniel Wylde.' He could do nothing less than offer his own name, though he did not add the title.

The other man did it for him. 'You are the Earl of Montcliffe? I saw the insignia upon your carriage outside and Mr Tattersall himself pointed your personage out to me here last week as a man who knows his way around a horse.'

'Indeed.' Even with the frosty tone of the reply Cameron seemed unfazed.

'My greys are this way, my lord. Would you do me the honour of looking them over?'

'I am not in the market for a purchase.' Hell and damnation, there was no untruth in that, he thought, his hands fisting in his pockets with the sort of rage he had almost become accustomed to. Noticing others looking his way, Daniel tried to soften his face.

'But you are renowned for your knowledge of a fine buy in horseflesh and it is that I seek to be assured of. I was only hoping for the chance of an expert's opinion.'

They had passed beneath the roof delineating the courtyard now and had wandered down into the stables proper. It was darker here and a lot less busy. When the ground unexpectedly fell away the old man tripped, Daniel's arm steadying him before he lost balance completely.

'Thank you, my lord.' Cameron's voice was quieter and the flesh beneath the finely made coat felt alarmingly thin. Life had honed his instincts and Daniel's were on high alert. This man was not quite as he seemed and he wondered at what was hidden.

'Here they are. Maisey and Mick. After my parents, you understand, though they will not be billed as such here. Names of high distinction fetch more in the way of coinage, I am told, and so Mr Tattersall thinks to call them after ancient Grecian gods.'

The greys were of Arabian descent, their distinctive head shapes and high-tailed carriage unmistakable. The horses were small and refined, and Daniel could have picked their lineage out easily from a thousand others.

'Richard Tattersall is a shrewd operator so perhaps you should listen to what he says if you wish to part with them. I know my brother always paid through the nose here,' Daniel remarked.

Gnarled fingers were held against the jibbah bulge on the horse's forehead, and it was easy to see that there was no lack of love between the animal and its master as the horse nuzzled closer.

'Maisie finds any change difficult.' The catch in his voice suggested he did too.

'Why are you selling them, then? If you bred them, you could turn a tidy profit without too much work in it. A few years and the money could be double what a sale now would garner.'

'Time is a commodity I am a little short on, my lord.' The reply was grave. 'But you sound like my daughter.'

'The woman in the carriage?' Why the hell had he said that? He wished he might take such a question back.

'My beautiful jewel.'

Again Daniel was shocked. In his circle it was not done to talk of progeny in such glowing terms.

'Are you married, my lord?' Another impertinence. Did Mr Robert Cameron always speak without thought?

'No. Too busy saving England.' He knew he should adopt a sterner demeanour, but the man was beguiling in his lack of protocol. The memory of a soldier he had once known came to mind. A man who had served with him and saved his life before losing his own on the high hills of Penasquedo. He shook away ennui. Of late the emotion seemed to have hitched a ride upon his shoulders, crouching over everything he said and did; a result of the problems at Montcliffe Manor probably and the cursed debts that had piled up in the years between his father's indifference and his brother's high-stakes gambling.

The other looked relieved at his answer.

'A parent would do almost anything to keep a child happy, you understand?'

'Indeed, I should imagine such a thing to be so.'

'I would give my horses without a moment's hesitation to a husband who had the wherewithal to make my girl smile.'

'A generous gift.' Where was this conversation leading? Daniel wondered, as a small seed of worry began to grow.

'I was married myself for twelve long and happy years before my wife passed on. Well before her time too, I should say, and for a while…' He stopped and brought out a large white kerchief to dab his face with. 'For a while I thought to follow. The world is a lonely place to be without the love of a good woman and it was the nights that were the worst.' Shrewdness lurked above sorrow in Robert Cameron's eyes.

The stallion had now come over for its share of attention and Daniel had seldom seen another of its ilk; leanly muscled and compact, he was built for endurance, head turned towards him and darkly intelligent eyes watchful. If he had had the money he would have placed it down right then and there because he knew without a doubt that offspring from these two would soon be worth a small fortune on any market in the world.

'Where did you get them?'

'In Spain. Near Bilbao. I had heard of them and went over to look. Fell in love at first glance and brought them back three years ago.'

'Don't sell them cheap, then. If you hold out for your price, their worth will be increased,' Daniel advised.

'You wouldn't be interested in purchasing them yourself?'

This was not said with any intention at rudeness. It was just a passing comment, a friendly gesture to a stranger. Of course Cameron would think the Montcliffe coffers full. Everybody still did.

He shook his head. If he could have raised

the money, he would have bid for the pair in a trice, but that sort of life was finished and had been for a while now. He noticed a few other patrons drifting down to take a look at the greys. And then more came. However, Robert Cameron did not seem the slightest bit interested in singing the praises of his horseflesh any longer which was surprising, given the hard line he had taken just a moment before.

As the crowds thickened Daniel tipped his hat at the timber merchant and made his way out of the crush.

Three-quarters of an hour later, he was glad to sit down on the comfortable seat of his carriage. His right leg ached today more than it had in months and he knew that the bullet would have to be removed before too much longer. The Montcliffe physician had told him that time and time again, but the worry of being left a cripple was even worse than the pain that racked through him each time he stepped on it.

Throwing his hat on the seat, Daniel leant back into the leather and ran his fingers through his hair. It was too damn long and he would cut it tonight after a bath. His valet had once done the job, but Daniel had let him go, as he had had to do with other staff both at the town house and at Montcliffe.

He cursed Nigel again as he did almost every day now, his brother's lack of care of the family inheritance beyond all comprehension. One should not think ill of the dead, he knew, but it was hard to find generous thought when any new debt now joined the pile of all the others.

A sudden movement caught his attention and he focused on a group in a narrow alleyway off Hyde Park Corner. Four or five men circled around another and it was with a shock that he realised the one in the middle was the timber merchant, Mr Robert Cameron.

Banging on the roof of the conveyance, he threw open the door and alighted quickly as it stopped. Twenty paces had him amidst the ruckus and he saw the old man's nose streamed with blood.

'Let him go.' Raising his cane, he brought it down hard on the hand of the man closest to him as the scoundrel reached inside his coat for something. A howl of pain echoed and a knife dropped harmlessly to the cobbles, spinning on its own axis with the movement.

'Anyone else want a try?' He knew he had the upper hand as the thugs backed off, yelling obscenities at him, but nothing else. They were gone before he counted to ten and there was only silence in the street.

Cameron was leaning over as though in pain, his right arm held to his chest.

'What hurts?'

'My...pride.' As he straightened Daniel saw the grimace on his face.

'Did you know them?'

The older man nodded. 'They have been demanding money from me.'

'Why?'

'My business is lucrative and they want a slice. One of their number also used to work for me in the warehouse until I fired him for stealing and I suspect he holds a grudge.' He dabbed at his nose with his dislodged shirt tails. 'If you had not come...'

'I will take you home if you give me your direction.'

As Cameron was about to argue Daniel called his driver down from the high seat to give a hand and ten minutes later they were pulling up in front of a large town house in Grosvenor Square.

No little fortune here then, Daniel thought, as he helped Cameron out. He noticed blood had left a stain on the leather seat at about the same time as the other did.

'If you wait, I will find coinage to cover the cost of the cleaning.'

'It is of no significance.'

Cameron was now leaning on him heavily and he could feel the shaking of fright beginning to settle. As they came to the front door the sound of running feet was heard.

'Are you hurt?' Worry coated the voice of the woman who came into view, the same woman he had seen in the carriage, anger on her face creasing it badly. Cameron's daughter by his own admission, though she looked nothing at all like him.

'What on earth happened?' She reached his side and all but pulled her father out of Daniel's grasp, the sharp edge of a fingernail carving skin away from his wrist. If she noticed, she did not show it, merely helping her father backwards to a sofa that was perched to one side of the wide lobby.

'Sit down. You look blue around the mouth.' Her own mouth was a tight line of consternation, her dark eyes flashing up at Daniel in question. 'Who did this?'

'A group of blackguards waylaid him not far from Tattersall's.'

'You did not wait for the carriage, Papa. You said to send it at two, did you not?' As if on cue the big clock in another corner struck the half hour of one-thirty.

'I h-had done all I needed to at the auction house.'

'You sold the horses?' A new tone entered her voice, one of censure and irritation. Lord, the girl was a harpy and with no introduction Daniel was hard pressed to say anything.

Robert Cameron was shaking his head and looking worse by the moment. 'The Earl of Montcliffe here helped me and brought me home. Lord Montcliffe, may I present my daughter, Amethyst Amelia Cameron, to you.'

Amethyst? His jewel? She did not suit such a name at all with her dark eyes and angry mouth. Her hair was a strange lustreless brown pulled back into a bun that was fashioned in the most unflattering of styles.

As if she could read his mind her expression tightened and she barely acknowledged the introduction. The clothes she wore were serviceable homespun without embellishment. The sort of dress one might wear to a dowdy funeral, the cloth of black showing up her skin as sallow and underlining the smudged circles beneath her eyes as dark bruises.

She was not a beauty, but she was not plain either. Beneath the downcast glance he caught a flash of anger, abrupt and sudden.

Tipping his head at her, he was surprised when she flushed a bright beet red, though she looked away, ringing for the butler to fetch a physician immediately.

Efficient and calm now, save for the remaining stain of red on her cheeks which made her look vulnerable. He wanted to lay his hand upon her arm and tell her...what? He shook the thought away and concentrated on her father, whose eyes were glued to his daughter, a speculative glance within them.

'I hope you will recover without any ill effects, sir,' Daniel said. 'If you wish to take such an assault further with the law and need verification of exactly what I saw, you may call on me.'

Extracting his card from a thin leather holder in his pocket, he handed it over.

'Thank you for your help, Lord Montcliffe, I have appreciated it greatly.'

Acknowledging the gratitude, Daniel turned

to leave, though the daughter, after fumbling in a drawer to one side of the room, came forth with a wad of bank notes.

'I hope this might help in the way of thanks.' Her voice was no longer shrill, but the insult of payment was all Daniel could think of.

Without another word he turned and walked from the room, the butler hurrying to show him the way out.

'Perhaps I insulted him, Papa, by offering him reimbursement for his trouble?' Amethyst looked down at the substantial sum in her hands. Every other member of her acquaintance would have taken it and with the thankfulness that was intended, but not the Earl of Montcliffe.

She was irritated with herself for allowing such an awkward meeting, but she had been more than surprised to see the man outside the Tattersall's auction rooms right here in their town house. She knew Lord Montcliffe had noticed her embarrassment and she chastised herself for even thinking of giving him reimbursement for a deed of honour.

Such a reward belittled the act, she supposed, by reducing it to terms of cold hard cash.

She had heard that the *ton* rarely even carried money, the tarnish of trade and commerce resting instead with their accompanying helpers and sycophants.

Traders and merchants. Even with a princely sum made from hard work, good luck and risky ventures, the Camerons would not be accepted into any of the higher echelons of society.

Well, she could not care. No doubt Lord Montcliffe would be mulling over his encounter with them on the carriage ride home before sharing the story of her clumsy attempt at recompense with his peers at some exclusive 'members only' club in the nicer areas of the city. She was so very glad he was gone.

'You need to inform the constabulary of this assault, Papa. You cannot keep pretending that this matter will simply disappear.'

'You think I should pay them?' For the first time ever Amethyst heard a tone in her father's voice that suggested complete uncertainty and she did not like it at all.

'No, of course not. Pay once and they will haunt us indefinitely. These people need to be cut off at the roots.'

Her father laughed. 'Sometimes, Amethyst, you are so like your mother that it brings tears to my eyes.' He took in a breath. 'But if Susannah were here I think she would be scolding me for involving you so much in the business that you have forgotten about living.' The handkerchief pressed to his nose still showed blood appearing through the thickness of the layers of cotton and Amethyst hoped that the physician might hurry. 'A man like Montcliffe would make you smile again.'

'I am quite happy as I am, Papa, and as Montcliffe must have every single woman's heart in London a-racing he would hardly be interested in mine.'

The strange glint in his eyes was worrying for Amethyst knew her father well enough to know just what that meant.

She wandered across to the mews behind the house after her father had retired. Robert had bought in this particular area in London because of the proximity of the stables that held enough room to house livestock.

The stablemaster, Ralph Moore, was just finishing brushing down Midnight, a large black stallion her father had acquired in the past year.

'It is a sad day when the cream of our livestock is left to languish in the Tattersall's stable on view for sale, Miss Cameron. I know it is not my place to criticise anything your father does and he has been a kind and mindful master, but with a bit of patience and some good luck the greys could be the start of a line of horses England has not seen the likes of before. I have spoken of it with him, but he does not want to even consider such a proposition any longer.'

Such words made Amethyst wary. Why would her father suddenly not want the pleasure of breeding his Arabian pair, something he had always spoken of with much anticipation and delight?

Tonight she felt restless and uncertain and the dangerous beauty of Lord Montcliffe came to mind. She wished she had not blushed so ridiculously when he had looked across at her or seen the returning humour in his eyes. The heat of shame made her scalp itch and, reaching up, she snatched the offending wig from her head and shook out the short curls beneath it, enjoying the freedom.

It was finally getting longer. Almost six inches now. Curlier than it had ever been and a much lighter colour. Soon she would be able to dispense with the hairpiece altogether.

If she had been at Dunstan, she would have

saddled up one of the horses and raced towards the far hills behind the house. Here in London the moon was high and full, tugging at her patience, stretching the limit of her city manners, making her feel housebound and edgy.

A noise had her turning.

'When I could not find you I knew you would be here.'

Her father joined her at the side of Midnight's stall, Ralph Moore's departure a few moments prior to his room upstairs allowing them privacy. Her father's left eye was darkened and his nose swollen.

'I imagined you would have gone up to bed early after such a dreadful day,' she said.

'Slumber is harder to find as the years march on.' His glance rose to her hair. 'It is nice to see you without the ugly wig, my love, for your skin appears a much better colour without it.'

Shaking her head, Amethyst looked down at the limp brown hairpiece in her hands. 'I should have a new one ordered, I suppose, but it seems so frivolous for the small amount of time I still have need of it.'

'Well, it is good to see you happier, my dear. Perhaps the exchange with Lord Montcliffe has given you some vitality? He is a good man and strong. Mr Tattersall spoke of him highly as a lord who can be relied upon.'

'Relied on to do what?'

'To look after you. I shall not be around for ever and...'

His sentiments petered away as she began to laugh out loud. 'I hardly think that was what Mr Tattersall was referring to. Besides, an exalted lord of the realm would have no mind to mingle with a woman from trade.'

'But if he did, my love, would you have the inclination to consider him as a husband?'

'Husband?' Now all humour fled. 'My God, Papa, you cannot be serious for he would never marry me. Not for all the gold in England. Men like Lord Montcliffe marry women exactly like them. Rich. Beautiful. Young. Well connected. Debutantes who have a world of possibilities at their feet.'

Her father shook his head. 'I disagree with you. Your mother taught me that those things are not the most important qualities to ensure the success of a union. She said that a partner with an alert and interested mind is worth much more than one of little thought or originality. Besides, we have accrued enough money to lure even the loftiest of the lords of the *ton*.'

His words seeped into her astonishment. 'Why are you saying these things, Papa? Why would you be even thinking of them? I am a widow and I am almost twenty-seven years old. My chances of such marital bliss are long since passed and I have accepted that they are.'

In the moonlight her father's face looked older and infinitely sadder. As he leant forward to take her hand Amethyst felt her heart lurch in worry, the certainty of what he was about to tell her etched into fright.

Midnight's breath in the moonlight, the call of an owl far off in the greenness of the park, a carriage wending its way home along Upper Brook Street at the end of another busy night. The sounds of a normal and ordinary late evening, everything in place, settling in and waiting for the dawn, allowing all that had happened through the day to be assimilated by a gentle darkness.

The far edge of happiness is here, Amethyst thought. *Here, before the crack of change opens up to swallow it.* She knew what he would say for she could see it in his eyes.

'I am seriously unwell, my dear. The doctor does not expect my heart to last out the year in the shape it is in. He advised me to settle my affairs and make certain everything is in order.'

Worse than a crack. An abyss unending and deep. Her hands closed about his, the chill in his thin fingers underlying everything. She could not even negate all he said and the reply she was about to give him was driven into silence by fear.

'My one and only prayer is that the Lord Above in His Infinite Wisdom might grant me the promise of knowing you are safe, Amethyst. Safe and married to a man who would not forsake you. Lord Montcliffe is the first man I have seen you look at since Gerald Whitely. He is well regarded by everyone who knows him and it is rumoured that his financial position is somewhat shaky. We could help him.'

Stop, she should have said. Stop all this nonsense now. But in the shafts of light she registered something in her father's eyes that she had not seen in a long, long time. Hope, if she could name it; hope of a future for her, even if he was not in it.

The gift of a place and a family, that was what he was trying to give her. There was no thought of greed or power or station. No inkling of a crazed want to surge up the social ladder, either. It was only his love that fostered such thoughts.

'Would you listen with your intellect to what I have to ask you, my love, and perhaps your heart as well?' he asked.

As much as she wanted to shake her head and tell him to stop, she found herself acquiescing.

'There is only us now, the last of the Camerons, and the world is not an easy place to be left alone. I want you to be guarded and cared for by an honourable man, a man who would ward away danger. I want this more than I have ever wanted anything in my life before, Amethyst. If I knew you were safe, it would mean I could enjoy what is left of my life in peace. If I could go to your mother in Heaven and know that I had done my very best to keep you protected, then I would be a happy man. Susannah instructed me to see you lived well in her last breath of life and if it is the final thing that I can do for her then, by God, I am willing to try.'

Crack. Crack crack. Like ice on a winter lake, Amethyst's heart was breaking piece by piece as he spoke.

Chapter Two

'There is someone to see you, Lord Montcliffe. A tradesman by the name of Mr Robert Cameron and he is most insistent that he be allowed to come inside.'

'Send him in.'

'Through the front door, my lord?' His butler's tone was censorious.

'Indeed.'

'Very well, my lord.'

It had been a couple of weeks since the *contretemps* at Hyde Park Corner and Daniel wondered what on earth Cameron might want from him. The Arabian greys had been pulled from auction the day after they had last spoken and the small bit of investigation he had commissioned on the character of the man had been most informative.

Mr Robert Cameron was a London merchant who was well heeled and wily. He owned most of the shares in a shipping line trading timber between England and the Americas, his move into importing taking place across the past eight or so years, and he was doing more than well.

However, when the door opened again and Cameron came through, Daniel was shocked.

The man of a little over a fortnight ago was thinner and more pallid, the bruising around his eyes darker.

'Thank you for seeing me, Lord Montcliffe.' Cameron waited as the servant departed the room, peering about to see no others lingered in the background of the substantial library. 'Might I speak very frankly to you and in complete confidence, my lord?'

Interest flickered. 'You may, but please take a seat.' He gestured to the leather wingchair nearby for Cameron looked more than unsteady on his feet.

'No. I would rather stand, my lord. There are words I need to say that require fortitude, if you will, and a sitting position may lessen my resolve.'

Daniel nodded and waited as the other collected himself. He could think of no reason whatsoever for the furtive secrecy or the tense manner of the man.

'What I am about to offer, Lord Montcliffe, must not leave the confines of this room, no matter what you might think of it. Will you give me your word as a gentleman on that whether you accept my proposal or not?'

'It isn't outside of the law?'

'No, my lord.'

'Then you have my word.'

'Might I ask for a drink before I begin?'

'Certainly. Brandy?'

'Thank you.'

Pouring two generous glasses, Daniel passed one over, waiting as the older man readied himself to speak.

'My health is not as it was, my lord. In fact, I think it fair to say that I am not long for this world.' He held up his hand as Daniel went to interrupt. 'It is not condolences I am after, my lord. I only tell you this because the lack of months left to me owe a good part to what I propose to relate to you next.'

Taking a deep swallow of his brandy, Cameron wiped his mouth with his hands. Labourers hands with wide calluses and small healed injuries. The hands of someone used to many long hours of manual work.

'I want to bequeath the pair of greys to you, my lord. I know you will love them in the same manner as I do and that they will not be sold on, so to speak, for a quick financial profit. Mick and Maisie need a home that will nurture them and I have no doubts you shall do just that. I would also prefer their names to stay just as they are as the Grecian ones suggested by Mr Tattersall didn't appeal to me at all.'

'I could not accept such an offer, Mr Cameron, and have not the means to buy them from you at this moment. Besides, it is unheard of to give a complete stranger such a valuable thing,' Daniel replied, taken aback.

For the first time Cameron smiled. 'But you see, my lord, I can do just as I will. Great wealth produces a sense of egocentricity and allows a freedom that is undeniable. I can bequeath anything I like to anybody I want and I wish for you to have my greys.'

Daniel tried to ignore the flare of excitement that started building inside him. With such horses he could begin to slowly recoup a little of the family fortune by running a breeding programme at Montcliffe Manor that would be the envy of society. But he stopped himself. There had to be a catch here somewhere, for by all accounts Cameron was a shrewd businessman and a successful one at that.

'And in return?'

'Your estate is heavily mortgaged and I have it on good authority that a hefty loan your brother took out with the Honourable Mr Reginald Goldsmith will be called in before the end of this month. He had other outstanding loans as well and I have acquired each and every one to do just as I will with them.'

'What is your meaning?' Daniel bit out, forcing himself to stand still.

'Coutts is also worried by your lack of collateral and, given the Regent's flagrant dearth of care with his finances, they are now beating a more conservative pathway in the management of their long-term lending. With only a small investigation I think you might find yourself in trouble.'

'You would ruin me?'

'No, my lord, exactly the opposite. I wish to gift you three sums of twenty-five thousand pounds each year for the next three years and then the lump sum of one-hundred-and-fifty thousand pounds.'

A fortune. Daniel could barely believe the proportions of the offer, such riches unimaginable.

'I would immediately sign over the town house in Grosvenor Square as an incentive for you to honour the terms. Then, whenever Amethyst instructs me to do so, a property I own to the north called Dunstan House, with a good deal of acreage about it, shall be endorsed into your care, as well.'

Stopping, the merchant faced him directly. Sweat had built on his brow and his cheeks were marked with a ruddy glow of much emotion. 'There is one thing, however, that you must do for me in return, my lord. My only daughter Amethyst is now twenty-six, soon to be twenty-seven. She is a clever girl and a sensible one. She has worked alongside me for the last eight years and it is her surefootedness in business that has propelled my profits skywards.'

He waited as Daniel nodded before continuing.

'Amethyst Amelia was educated under the capable tutelage of the Gaskell Street Presbyterian Church School and I paid the teachers handsomely to make sure that she acquired all the skills a woman of the classes above her might need to know. In short, she could fit into any social situation without disgracing herself.'

Daniel suddenly knew just where this conversation was leading to. A dowry. A bribe. The answer to his prayers for the selling of his soul.

'You are single and available, my lord. You have two sisters who are in need of being launched into society, a mother who has fine taste in living and a grandfather who requires much in the way of medical attention. All continuing and long-term expenses. If you marry my daughter by the end of July, none of this will ever be a problem again and you will have the means to right the crumbling estate of Montcliffe once and for all.'

'Get out, you bastard.' Daniel's anger made the words tremble. That a man he was beginning to respect and like should think of coming into his life to blackmail him into marrying his daughter. For that was what this was. Blackmail, even given the enormous amounts mooted.

But Cameron looked to be going nowhere. 'I can understand your wrath and indeed, were I in your boots, I might have had exactly the same reaction. But I would ask you to think about it for at least a week. You have promised me your confidence and I expect that, for if a word of this gets out anywhere my daughter's reputation will be ruined. Hence, as a show of my own gratitude for your discretion, I shall leave you the greys regardless of your final decision.'

'I cannot accept them.'

'Here is a document I have written up for your perusal and I earnestly hope to hear from you presently.'

With that he was gone, his glass emptied on the desk and a fat envelope left beside it. Daniel was in two minds as to what to do: send it back unopened with a curt message containing his lack of interest or open it up and see what was inside.

Curiosity won out.

The sheet before him was witnessed by a city lawyer whose qualifications seemed more than satisfactory. It was also signed by his daughter.

'Damn. Damn. Damn.' He whispered the words beneath his breath. The girl had been told of all this and still wanted the travesty? Finishing his brandy, he poured himself another as he read on, barely believing what was written.

He was to marry Amethyst Amelia Cameron

before the month was finished on the condition that he have no relations with any other woman for two years afterwards.

Shocked to the core, he took a good swallow of the brandy. Amethyst Amelia Cameron would allow her father to sell her for the promise of what? Under the law any daughter could inherit money, chattels and unentailed property from a dying father and he obviously loved her. Besides, she had experience in the business and had turned profits for many a year. Cameron had told him that himself. So what was it that she would gain from such an arrangement? They barely knew each other and, even given she was from the trading classes, an heiress of her calibre could garner any number of titled aristocrats who were down on their purse.

As he was?

'Hell!' Daniel threw the parchment into a drawer and slammed it shut, but the promises festered even unseen, malevolent and beguiling.

How on earth had Cameron known so much about his financial difficulties? Would Goldsmith truly call in his brother's loans against Montcliffe before he was ready for them? If he did that, Daniel would be forced to sell the town house, the manor, the surrounding farms and any chattels that would fetch something. Then the Wyldes would be homeless, money-lenders baying for their blood and all the claws unsheathed.

If it was just him, he might have been able to manage, but Cameron was perfectly correct; his sisters were young, his grandfather was old and his mother had always found her gratification in the position the earldom afforded them in society and had freely spent accordingly.

Standing, he walked to the window and looked out over the gardens, swearing as he saw the two greys tied to a post by the road-side and his butler near them, looking more than bewildered.

He had left them just as he'd said. It was begun already. Daniel turned to the doorway and hurried through it.

'I think he took my proposal very well.' Robert Cameron sipped at the sweet tea Amethyst had brought him and smiled.

'You do?'

'He is a good man with sound moral judgement and a love for his family.'

Amethyst bit into a ginger biscuit, wiping the crumbs away from her lips.

'So he signed his name to the deed?'

'Not quite.'

'He didn't sign it?'

Her father looked up. 'He told me that I was a bastard for even suggesting such a thing and said that I should get out.'

'But you left the greys?'

'I did.'

'And he has as yet not sent them back?'

'He has not.'

'Then it is a good omen.'

Robert frowned. 'I hope so, Amethyst, I really do.'

Amethyst tried her hardest to smile. Papa had become thinner and thinner no matter what she might get their French chef to feed him and he had taken to striding about the house at night...watching. He was scared and those that might harm them for their money were becoming braver. The daylight attack near Tattersall's had made her father paranoiac about any movement in their street, any unknown face around the warehouse. Nay, he was eating himself up with worry and she could allow it no longer.

Papa wanted her to be protected and he desperately wanted her to trust in a man again. With time running out for her father Amethyst had allowed him the choice of her groom. Said like that it sounded abhorrent, but nothing was ever as black and white as one might imagine and right now she wanted her father to smile.

'We shall wait a week. If Lord Montcliffe has not come back to us by then with an answer, we will visit him together.' She injected a jaunty positive note into her words but everything in her felt flat.

Gerald Whitely's face shimmered in her memory. The feel of his anger was still there sometimes, just beyond touch, his angry words and then his endless seething silence. A relationship that had blinded sense and buried reason, one bad decision following another until there was nothing left of any of it.

Cold fingers closed over the cross at her throat. Her father was the one person who had stayed constant in her life and she would do whatever it took to see that he was happy. Anything at all.

'Your mother made me promise to see you flourish, Amy. They were the last words she spoke to me as she slipped away and I had hoped that you would, but after Whitely…' He stopped, his voice wavering and frighteningly thin. 'Lord Montcliffe will make you remember to laugh again. He loves horses and they love him back. Any man who can win the trust of an animal is a good man, an honest man, and I can see that in him when I look him in the eyes.'

She hoped her smile did not appear false as he held her hand, the dearness of the gesture so familiar.

'Promise me you will try to give him all your heart, body and soul, Amethyst. No reservations. It is how your mama loved me and there is no defence for a man against a woman like that. Such strength only allows growth and wonder between a married couple and I know you have been saddened by love…'

She shook his words away, the reminder of bitterness unwanted. Her choice, cankered before it had even begun.

'When death claimed Gerald Whitely, my love, I was not sorry. Sense tells me that you were not either.'

So he knew of that? Another shame. A further deceit that had not remained hidden.

'It was the Cameron fortune Gerald was after, Papa. Perhaps Lord Montcliffe and he are not so unalike after all?'

But her father shook his head. 'Whitely fashioned his own demise. Daniel Wylde is only trying to clean up after the mistakes of his brother and father and is doing so to protect the family he has left.'

'A saint, then?' She wished that the caustic undertone in her words was not quite so unmistakable.

'Hardly. But he is the first man you have given a second glance to. The first man who has made you blush. Such attraction must account for something because it was the same with Susannah and me.'

Despite everything she smiled. 'I imagine that Lord Montcliffe has that effect upon everybody whoever meets him, Papa. I was not claiming him for myself.'

'Because you do not trust your judgements pertaining to the acquisition of a husband, given the last poor specimen?'

Her father had never before, in the year since his death, spoken of Gerald Whitely in this way. That thought alone lent mortification to her sinking raft of other emotions.

Failure. It ate at certainty like a large rat at a wedding feast. Once she had chosen so unwisely she felt at a loss to ever allow herself such a mandate again. Perhaps that was a part of the reason she did not rally against her father's arguments. That and the yellowing shades of sickness that hung in the whites of his eyes.

Death held a myriad of hues. Gerald's had been a pale and unholy grey when she had seen him laid out in the undertaker's rooms. Her mother's had been red-tinged, a rash of consequence marked into the very fabric of her skin and only fading hours after she had taken her final and hard-fought breath.

Amethyst's nails dug deep into her thighs as she willed such thoughts aside. A long time ago she had been a happier person and a more optimistic one. Now all she could manage was the pretence of it.

It was easier to allow Papa the hope of joy in his final months, the illusion of better times, of children, of the *'heart and body and soul'* love her father had felt for her mother and which he imagined was some sort of a God-given rite of passage. Once she had believed in such a thing as well, but no longer.

All she could muster now was a horror for anything that held the hint of intimacy.

Blemished. Damaged. Hurt.

Daniel Wylde would understand sooner or later the payment required for the Cameron fortune and she was sure he would feel every bit as cheated as she did. But at least Papa would go to his grave believing that his only daughter was safe and happy, the soldier earl he had chosen for her strong enough to ward off any threats of menace.

She leaned down and picked up a small coin from a collection on a plate, balancing it in her palm before flipping it over. *If it shows heads this marriage will work and if it does not…* When the coin fell to tails she chastised herself for playing such silly games.

When Daniel returned from an outing later in the day his mother was ensconced in the drawing room at the Montcliffe town house, a glass of his finest brandy in her hand and a thoughtful look upon her face.

'Have you been procuring new horseflesh, Daniel? There is a pair of magnificent greys in your stable and I just wondered…'

'They were a gift, Mother. I did not purchase them.'

'A gift? From whom?' The silk in the gown Janet, Lady Montcliffe, wore matched her eyes exactly, a deep sapphire blue. A new possession, he supposed, thinking of the demand for payment that would come across his desk before much longer.

He could have been truthful, could have simply stated that there was a possibility he would be married and that the greys had been a pre-wedding present, but something made him stop. Anger, he supposed, and shame and the fact that to voice such a thing might make it feel more real and true.

With the Camerons he felt removed from society. In their company the preposterous proposed union made a sort of skewed sense that it didn't here in front of his mother.

When he didn't answer, his mother remarked, 'Charlotte Hughes is back from Scotland. I saw her today at the Bracewells and she asked after you. She is looking a picture of health and wealth and was sporting a necklace with an emerald attached to it the size of a walnut.'

'I am no longer interested in Lady Mackay, Mama.' He stressed her married name.

'Well, she seemed more than interested in your whereabouts. She had heard of the fracas at La Corunna, of course, and was most concerned about the injury to your leg. There were tears in her eyes when I told her of it and such compassion is heartwarming.'

Daniel interrupted her. 'Is that my French brandy you are drinking?' Crossing to the cabinet, he found the bottle and frowned as he saw there was barely any left. His whole family had been falling apart for years. His mother with her drink, his brother with his gambling and his sisters with their brittle sense of entitlement and whining. Only his grandfather had seemed to hold it together, though his body was letting him down more and more often.

'If you are going to lecture me about the evils of strong drink...'

Daniel shook his head. 'This evening I cannot find the energy to do so. If you wish to kill yourself by small degrees with your misplaced grief for my brother's stupidity...'

'Nigel was a good boy...'

'Who mortgaged the Montcliffe property to the hilt as a payment for his escalating gambling habit.'

'He was trying to save the estate. He was trying to make everything right again,' she insisted.

'If you believe that, Mama, then you are as deluded as he was.'

His mother finished the glass of brandy and stood. 'The military campaign in Spain and Portugal has made you different, Daniel. Harder. A man of distance and callousness and I do not like what you have become.'

The sound of screams on a march from Hell with winter eating up any hope for warmth. Dead soldiers stripped of clothes and boots by others needing cover in the middle of a relentless freeze, and hundreds of miles left to reach the coast and to safety. Aye, distance came easily with such memories.

'In less than six months the Montcliffe properties will be bankrupt.'

He had not meant to say it like this, so baldly, and as his mother paled a compassion he had long since let go of spiked within.

'I have tried to tell you before, Mother. I have tried to make you understand that Nigel finished what our father started, but I can no longer afford to say it kindly. The estate lies precariously on the edge of insolvency.'

'You lie.'

'The bank won't lend the Montcliffe estate another penny and I have been warned that Goldsmith could call in one of Nigel's outstanding loans before the end of this month.'

'But Gwendolyn is to be presented in court and all the invitations to a soirée are written out. Besides, I have also just ordered several ball dresses from Madame Soulier. I cannot possibly curtail. If I do, others shall know of our plight and we shall suffer a very public shaming. Why, I could not even bear such a thing.'

Turning, Daniel held his breath, the guilt of Nigel's death eating at his equanimity. Years ago they had been close and he wondered if his time away from England in the army had left his brother exposed somehow. Lord knew his mother and sisters were unremitting in their demands. If he had been here, would he have been able to bolster Nigel's will and made him stronger, allowing him a sounding board for good sense and bolder decisions in the economic welfare of Montcliffe?

Taking a deep breath, he faced his mother directly. 'There is only one way that I can see of navigating the Montcliffe inheritances out of this conundrum.'

His mother wiped the tears from her eyes and looked up at him. He had never seen her appear quite as old and lined.

'How?'

'I can marry into money.'

'Old money?' Even under duress his mother remained a snob.

'Or money earned from the toil of hard labour and lucky breaks.'

'Trade?' The word was whispered with all the undercurrents of a shout.

'The alternative is bankruptcy,' he reminded her grimly.

'You have someone in mind?'

He could not say it, could not toss Amethyst Amelia Cameron's name into the ring of fire his mother had so effortlessly conjured up, a sneer on her lips and distaste in her blue eyes.

'Your father would be turning in his grave at such a suggestion. Marry one of the Stapleton girls, they would have you in a second, or the oldest Beaumont chit. She has made no secret of setting her cap at you.'

'Enough, Mother.'

'Charlotte Hughes, then, despite her foolish marriage. She has always loved you and you had strong feelings for her once. Besides, she is a lot more flush these days…'

'Enough.' This time he said it louder and she stopped.

'You have no true understanding of the difficulties that face me, Daniel…'

Her words were slightly slurred and he interrupted her. 'Your line in the sand is in danger of being washed away by strong drink, Mother, and it would help if you listened rather than argued. If you made some sacrifice in the family spending and pared down on the number of dresses and bonnets and boots you required, we may have some ready cash to tide us over whilst I try to extricate us from this Godforsaken mess.'

Already she was shaking her head. Sometimes he wondered why he had not just left and taken ship to the Americas, leaving the lot of them to wallow in the cesspool of their own making.

But blood and duty were thicker than both fury and defeat and so he had stayed, juggling what was left of the few assets against what had been lost into the wider world of debt.

If Goldsmith was to foreclose as Cameron had intimated he would? He shook away the dread.

So far he had not needed to sell any of the furniture or paintings in the London town house and so the effect of great wealth remained the illusion it always had been.

The avenues of escape were closing in, however, and he knew without a doubt that it was weeks rather than months for any monies left in the coffers to be gone. Nay, Cameron's option of a marriage of convenience was the only way to avoid complete ruin.

Upending her glass, his mother called her maid, heavily relying on the guiding arm of her servant as she stood.

'I shall speak with you again when you are less unreasonable.' The anger in her voice resonated sharply.

Brandy, arrogance and hopelessness. A familiar cocktail of Wylde living that had taken his father and brother into the afterlife too early.

He wondered if he even had the strength to try to save Montcliffe.

He met Lady Charlotte Mackay four days later as he exited the bank where he had spent an hour with the manager, trying to piece together some sort of rescue plan allowing the family estate a few more months of grace. And failing. His right leg hurt like hell and he had barely slept the night before with the pain of it.

Charlotte looked just as he remembered her, silky blonde curls falling down from an intricate hat placed high on her head. Her eyes widened as she saw it was he. Shock, he thought, or pity. These days he tried not to interpret the reaction of others when they perceived his uneven gait.

'Daniel.' Her voice was musical and laced with an overtone of gladness. 'It has been an age since I have seen you and I was hoping you might come to call upon me. I have been back from Edinburgh for almost a sennight and had the pleasure of meeting your mother a few days ago.'

'She mentioned she had seen you.'

'Oh.'

The conversation stopped for a second, the thousand things unsaid filling in the spaces of awkwardness.

'I wrote to you, of course, but you did not answer.' Her confession made him wary, and as her left hand came up to wipe away an errant curl from her face he saw her fingers were ringless.

He could have said he had not received any missives and, given the vagaries of the postal system, she would have believed him. But he didn't lie.

'Marriage requires a certain sense of loyalty, I have always thought, so perhaps any communication between us was not such a good idea.'

Small shadows dulled the blue of her irises. 'Until a union fails to live up to expectation and the trap of a dreary routine makes one's mind wander.'

Dangerous ground this. He tried to turn the subject. 'I heard your husband was well mourned at his funeral.'

'Death fashions martyrs of us all.' Her glance was measured. 'Widowhood has people behaving with a sort of poignant carefulness that is... unending and a whole year of dark clothes and joylessness has left me numb. I want to be normal again. I am young, after all, and most men find me attractive.'

Was this a proposition? The bright gown she wore was low-cut, generous breasts nestling in their beds of silk with only a minimal constraint. As she leaned forward he could not help but look.

The maleness in him rose like a sail in the wind, full of promise and direction, but he had been down this pathway once before and the wreck of memory was potent. He made himself stand still.

'I have learnt much through the brutal consequences of mistakes, but I am home alone tonight, Daniel. If you came to see me, we might rekindle all that we once had.'

Around them others hurried past, an ordinary morning in London, a slight chill on the air and the calling voices of street vendors.

He felt unbalanced by meeting her, given their last encounter. Betrayal was an emotion that held numerous interpretations and he hadn't cared enough to hear hers then.

But Charlotte Mackay's eyes now held a harder edge of knowledge, something war had also stamped on him. No longer simple. Two people ruined by the circumstances of their lives and struggling to hold on to anything at all. The disenchantment made him tired and wary and he was glad to see her mother hurrying towards them from the shop behind, giving no further chance of confidence.

Lady Wesley had changed almost as much as her daughter, the quick nervous laughter alluding to a nature that was teetering on some sort of a breakdown.

'My lord. I hope your family is all well?'

'Indeed they are, ma'am.'

'As you can see, our Charlotte is back and all in one piece from the wilds of Scotland.'

When he failed to speak she placed her arm across her daughter's. The suspicion that she was trying to transmit some hidden signal was underlined by the whitened skin over her knuckles. Charlotte looked suddenly beaten, the fight and challenge drained away into a vacuous smile of compliance.

Perhaps the Wesley family was as complex and convoluted as his own. Jarring his right foot, he swore to himself as they gave their goodbyes. His balance was worsening with the constant pain and the headache he was often cursed with was a direct result of that.

If the Camerons were to know the extent of his infirmity, would they withdraw their offer? Robert Cameron had told him that his daughter needed a strong husband. A protector. The beat of blood coursing around the bullet in his thigh was more distinct now just as the specialist he had seen last month had predicted it would become. If he left it too much longer, he would be dead.

The choice of the devil.

He had seen men in Spain and Portugal with

their limbs severed and their lives shattered. Even now in London the remnants of the rag-tag of survivors from the battlements of La Corunna still littered the streets, begging for mercy and succour from those around them.

He couldn't lose his leg. He wouldn't. Pride was one thing but so was the fate of his family. Dysfunctional the Montcliffes might be, but as the possessor of the title he had an obligation to honour.

For just a moment he wished he was back in Spain amongst his regiment as they rode east in the late autumn sunshine along the banks of the Tagus. The rhythm of the tapping drums and a valley filled with wildflowers came to mind, the ground soft underfoot and the cheers of the waving Spanish nationals ringing in his ears. A simple and uncomplicated time. A time before the chaos that was to be La Corunna. Even now when he smelt thyme, sage or lavender, such sights and sounds returned to haunt him.

The London damp encroached into his thoughts: the sound of a carriage, the calls of children in the park opposite. His life seemed to have taken a direction he was not certain of any more; too wounded to re-enlist, too encumbered by his family and its problems to simply disappear. And now a further twist—a marriage proposal that held nothing but compromise within it.

He tried to remember Amethyst Cameron's face exactly and failed in his quest. The dull brown of her hair, the wary anger in her eyes, a voice that was often shrill or scolding. The prospect of marriage to her was not what he had expected from his life, but in the circumstances what else could he do?

His eyes caught the movement of a little girl falling and scuffing her knees. An adult lifted her up and small arms entwined around the woman's neck, trusting, needing. Daniel imagined fatherhood would be something to be enjoyed, though in truth he had seldom been around any children. He turned away when he saw the woman watching him, uncertain perhaps of his intentions.

He was like a shadow, filled in by flesh and blood, but hurt by the empty spaces in his life. He wanted a wholeness again, a certainty, a resolve. He wanted to laugh as though he meant it and be part of something that was more than the shallow sum of his title.

If he did not marry Amethyst Amelia Cameron, the heritage of the Montcliffe name would be all but gone, a footnote in history, only a bleak reminder of avarice and greed. Centuries of lineage lost in the time it took for the bailiffs to eject the Wyldes from their birthright. The very thought of such a travesty made him hail a cabriolet. He needed to go home and read the small print and conditions of the Cameron proposal. He could not dally any longer.

A sort of calmness descended over the panic. His life and happiness would be forfeited, but there might be some redress in the production of a family. Children had no blame in the affairs of their parents and at thirty-three it was well past time that he produce an heir. An heir who would inherit an estate that was viable and in good health. An estate that would not be lost to the excesses of his brother or the indifference of his father.

Such a personal sacrifice must eventually come to mean something and he was damn well going to make certain that it did.

Chapter Three

The note came the seventh day after they had last seen him, a tense and formal missive informing them that Lord Daniel Wylde, the sixth Earl of Montcliffe, would be calling upon them at two in the afternoon.

Amethyst had been watching for him by the large bay window in the downstairs salon and she stiffened as she heard his carriage draw to a stop on the roadway in front of the house. Lord Montcliffe was here. She looked across at her father, his fingers knocking against his side in the particular way he had of showing concern. It did not help at all.

There were tea and biscuits already set out on the table and the finest of brandy in an unopened bottle. Every glass had been meticulously cleaned and snowy-white napkins stood at attention beside the plate of food, well ironed and folded.

'Lord Daniel Wylde, the Earl of Montcliffe, sir.' The butler used his sternest voice and made an effort not to look at anyone. Amethyst had instructed him on the exact art of manners before their guest had arrived.

And then the Earl was there, dressed in dark blue, the white cravat tied at his throat in the style of a man who hadn't put too much care into it. Not a fop or a dandy. She was pleased, at least, for that.

'Sir.' He looked at her father. 'Miss Cameron.' He did not even deign to glance her way, the anger on his brow eminently visible. The folder that Papa had made ready with the documents outlining the terms of their betrothal was in his hands. Each knuckle was stretched white. 'I accept.'

He threw the deeds on the table where they sat between the fine brandy and the fresh biscuits.

I accept.

Two words and she was lost into both method and madness; the Cameron fortune would remain intact and her own fate was sealed. For good or for bad. She felt her heart beating loud and heavy and, placing her hand on her breast, she pressed down, wanting this moment to stop and start again as something else.

But of course it did not.

'You accept?' Her father's voice was businesslike and brisk—a trader whose whole life had consisted of brokering arrangements.

The Earl nodded, but the expression on his face was stony. An agreement dragged from the very depths of his despair and nothing to be done about any of it. He knew as little of her as she did of him; two pawns in a game that was played for stakes higher than just their happiness alone. She had always known that, since the pounds had begun to roll into the Cameron coffers from the lucrative timber trade to and from the Americas. Great fortunes always came with a price.

'You have signed every condition, then?' Her father again. She thought he sounded just as he did when he was clinching a deal for the sale of a thousand yards of expensive American mahogany and she wondered at his calm and composure. She was his only daughter and again and again in her lifetime her father had insisted that she must marry for love.

Love? Unexpectedly she caught the eyes of

the Earl. Today the green was darker and distrusting. Still, even with the stark fury of coercion on his face, Daniel Wylde was the most beautiful man she had ever had the pleasure of looking upon.

Such looks would crucify her, for nobody would believe that he might have freely chosen her as his bride. She swallowed and met his glance. No use going to pieces this late in the game when the joy on her father's face was tangible. Papa had not appeared as happy for months.

'This is your choice too, Miss Cameron?'

'It is, my lord.' The floor beneath her began to waver, all the lies eliciting a sort of unreality that made her dizzy.

'You understand the meaning of the documents then?' he pressed.

'I do.' A blush crept up her throat as she thought of the clause stipulating the two years of monogamy. Her father's addition, that proviso, and though she had argued long and hard with him to remove it, Robert was not to be shifted.

Montcliffe turned away. The stillness she had noticed outside Tattersall's was magnified here, a man who knew exactly his place in the world and was seldom surprised by anything.

Save for this marriage of convenience.

'I hope then that the person you placed to look into my financial affairs can be trusted, Mr Cameron. If word were to leak out about my straitened circumstances and this unusual betrothal, I doubt I could protect your daughter from the repercussions.'

'Mr Alfred Middlemarch, my lawyer, is a model of silence, my lord. Nary a stray word shall be uttered.'

Their parlourmaid knocked timidly at the door, asking if she could come in to pour the tea. The Earl crossed the room to stand by the fireplace and chose brandy for his sustenance. When Hilda filled his glass to a quarter inch from the top Amethyst winced. On reflection, she thought, perhaps such a task was supposed to belong to the lady of the house and she wished she had not instructed the maid to return to do it. It was seldom that they had such lofty visitors and every small detail of service took on an importance that it previously never had.

Was this how she would live her life from now on? she wondered. On the edge of eggshells in case she were to inadvertently place a clumsy foot wrong? The tutors at Gaskell Street had tried their best with the vagaries of manners, but she imagined they had had about as much practice with the higher echelons of London society as she had.

To give Montcliffe some credit he sipped his tipple carefully from the top before placing the glass down on a green baize circle especially designed for such a purpose. She doubted her father had ever used them before, her eyes catching circles of darkness in the white oak where errant drinks had seeped into the patina of the wood.

Blemished, like them, the outward appearance of Papa and herself reflecting a life that had been lived in trade and service, with little time left for the niceties of cultured living. Amethyst wished she had at least gone out and bought a sumptuous dress for this occasion, something that might lift the colour of her skin into lustre.

She smiled at such a nonsense, catching the Earl's eyes again as she did so. When he looked away she saw that the muscle under his jaw quivered. In distaste? In sympathy? Usually she found people easy to read, but this man was not.

'I will announce our betrothal in *The Times* next week, if that is to your liking, Miss Cameron.'

So few days left?

'Thank you.' She wished her voice sounded stronger.

'I should not want a complicated ceremony given our circumstances.' A slight shame highlighted Daniel Wylde's cheeks after he said this and it heartened her immensely. He was not a man in the habit of being rude to women, then? She clutched at the cross at her throat and felt relieved.

Her father pressed on with his own ideas. 'I was thinking we might hold the ceremony here, my lord, with a minister from our Presbyterian church, of course, and any of your family and friends you care to invite. I would have the first of the money promised transferred into your bank account within the week.'

The give and the take of an agreement. Again Daniel Wylde looked at her as if waiting for her to speak. Did he imagine she might stand up and negate all that her father had so carefully planned? Montcliffe had seen just exactly what those who might hurt her father were capable of. Lord, she brought her hand up and felt the scar just beneath the heavy wig at her nape. It still throbbed sometimes in the cold and the headaches had never quite abated.

'After the nuptials we will repair to my family seat north of Barnet.'

'No!' It was the first real alarm Amethyst had felt. 'I need to be close to Papa and as he is retiring to Dunstan House then this is where I should like us to live…'

'I am certain we can work something out, my dear.' Her father now, placating such an outburst.

Again she shook her head, the pulse of her blood beating fast. 'I want to add a condition that I may live at Dunstan House, though if the Earl wishes to reside at Montcliffe Manor, then he may.'

'Difficult to fulfil the clause of mutual cohabitation for a full two years if that is the case, Miss Cameron.' His voice held a timbre of irony.

The clause her father had insisted upon. She glared at Robert, but kept her silence and was unexpectedly rescued by the very one she thought she would not be.

'It does not signify. We will reside wherever you wish to.' The Earl's tone was slightly bored. An unwanted wife. An unwelcomed cohabitation. Easier just to take the money and acquiesce.

'Then that is settled.' Her father, on the contrary, looked pleased with himself. The thought that perhaps he had over-exaggerated his own illness came to Amethyst's mind, but she dismissed this in the face of his extreme thinness. 'We shall ask if the children from Gaskell Street can be a part of the choir…'

'A small and simple wedding would be better, Papa.'

'I agree.' Lord Montcliffe spoke again. 'My family, however, are proponents of the High Anglican faith.'

'Then you bring your man of God and the service can be shared.' Papa had hit his stride now and the Earl looked to have no answer to such an unconventional solution. In fact, he looked plainly sick.

'A good solution, I think,' Robert went on to say. 'Then we can all be assured that you will be most properly married.' Standing after such a pronouncement, he walked to the door. 'But now I shall leave you alone for a few moments. I am sure there are things you might wish to say to one another without my presence to inhibit you.'

Amethyst glanced away, her father's words embarrassing and inappropriate. What could the Earl and she possibly have to talk about when there was a palpable distrust in the air? Usually Papa was more astute at reading the feelings of others and seldom acted in a manner that she found disconcerting.

When the door closed behind him, softly pulled shut inch by inch, Lord Montcliffe looked straight at her.

'Why would you agree to this charade, Miss Cameron?'

She asked him another question quickly back. 'Did you love your father, my lord?'

He looked perplexed as he answered, 'No.'

That threw her momentarily, but she made herself continue on. 'Well then, I think you must understand that I truly do love mine. Father, I mean.' Her voice shook. She was making a hash of this. 'Papa is ill and his one and only wish is to see me well protected and cared for. He is so ill that I fear—' She stopped, the words too shocking to say.

'Then why choose me in particular?' The tone of his fury was recognisable.

'You liked horses and you made it your business to save Papa from the attack in the alley when you could have so easily just gone on. I do not wish for a mean husband or an inconsiderate one, you understand. Also the army has made you strong. Another advantage, if you like.'

'A trade-off, then? Like the timber your father imports?'

'Exactly.' This was turning out to be a lot easier than she had hoped.

'Damn.' He swore and reached forward to tip her face up to his own.

'Are you truly as cold-blooded as that, Miss Cameron?' His green eyes narrowed as if he was listening for an answer and Amethyst was simply caught in the unexpected warmth of them. Paralysed. The darker green rim was threaded with gold.

'So there is no more to this agreement than the plain and blunt terms of commerce?' He let her go as she twisted away, uncertain of the words that he was saying and even more uncertain of her own reaction to them.

'If my father had not been ailing, I should not even be thinking of a betrothal, my lord, but he is fearful and fidgety and the doctor had made it clear that unless he relaxes and stops worrying…' She swallowed, her bottom lip wobbling. 'Your estate is falling into pieces about your feet and my father is dying. Our alliance should stave off the consequences of them both, yours for ever, and mine even for just a while. A business proposition, my lord, to suit us both.'

He turned away and walked to the window. No woman had ever spoken to him so plainly before. Usually the opposite sex fawned about him, the wiles of femininity well practised and honed and saying all that they thought he wished to hear.

Miss Amethyst Amelia Cameron seemed to possess none of these qualities and he was at a loss to know how to proceed.

'So I could have been anyone?'

When she did not answer, he added, 'Anyone with a dubious fiscal base and a strong military background?'

She looked over at him then with the directness that was so much part of her, a frown marring her forehead. 'You needed to be unmarried, of course, and not too old.' He was about to speak when she took a breath and carried on further. 'I also sincerely hope that I have not taken you from the arms of someone you love, for if that is the case I should absolve you from all the agreements between us. As a measure of good faith we would throw in the greys as a means to buy your silence on such a sensitive matter.'

He swore again and she flinched. The worth of the greys would not begin to cover the debts of Montcliffe.

'Why did you not choose a man you have some *tendre* for or one you had at least some notion of?' While she was being so brutally frank he thought he might at least discover something of the woman he would be tied to.

Her hand went to brush away the hair from around her face in a feminine and uncertain gesture. Against the window and in the light of a harsh afternoon sun she looked almost beautiful, a strong loveliness that was not much lauded in society these days, but one which caught at him in an unexpected twist of want. Not a woman of the same ilk as his sisters and mother with their constant neediness and fragility.

'There is no one else.' She did not even attempt platitudes.

Daniel had no experience of speaking with a

woman who would not be cowed by his title or by him personally and for one unlikely moment he thought he might tell her just that. With an effort he gathered himself together.

'Truth be told, Miss Cameron, I am caught in this ruse as certainly as you are.'

'Then perhaps it would be wise for us both to make the best of it. I would not hound you for much time or for sweet words, my lord, but what I would ask is that around my father you pretend a *tendre*, allowing him the contentment he deserves in what little is left of his life.'

'Would your mother have approved of you being such a martyr?'

A flash of anger came into her eyes, lighting the brown to a clear and brittle velvet. He was surprised by such a quick change. Not quite the demure woman he had imagined, after all. 'I think you forget, my lord, that I am as much a martyr to my family as you are to yours.'

'Touché.' Indeed she was right, the long line of Montcliffe ancestors all looking at him to save the Earldom for posterity. 'And if your father dies sooner rather than later, are the conditions within our marriage null and void?'

Her face crumbled into sheer distress. 'I sincerely pray that Papa should not succumb to his malady so readily, My lord. I should also impress upon you that putting aside a marriage so quickly would need to be most carefully handled.'

He almost laughed, thinking that she had no idea at all as to the whims of the *ton* in their dealings with the protection of large inheritances. Indeed, a hundred marriages that he knew of were conveniently forgotten about in the face of shapely courtesans and willing mistresses. Another thought also worried him. Perhaps in her circle of acquaintances such a truism was not as absolute.

He had never been a flagrant womaniser, but neither was he a man who would want to be bound for years in a union without love or respect.

When Robert Cameron came back into the room Daniel lost his chance to ask exactly what she thought to get from this alliance personally. Her father looked absurdly pleased with himself, a smile from one side of his face to the other.

'I hope you have been able to find out a little about each other. My Amethyst was the cleverest of all the young ladies at her school, my lord, and won the first prize for academic endeavour for her year.'

'I am certain he cannot be interested in such things, Papa, and—'

But Daniel did not allow her to finish. 'Rest assured, Mr Cameron, I am.'

Her father frowned and helped himself to a drink. His bride-to-be stood perfectly still, a statue before the windows, her lustreless hair caught in the shafts of sunlight as she warned her father off saying more. Another darker thought suddenly occurred to him.

'Have you had trouble with those who waylaid you before?'

Cameron looked at his daughter. God, Daniel thought, had Amethyst Cameron been hurt by the thugs too?

'The wheel of a carriage we were in sheared off just under a year ago because it had been cut almost right through,' she answered, the fright in her eyes visible. 'Our conveyance overturned a number of times and Papa and I were caught inside. We were out on business, you see, and those responsible knew we would be travelling on that road on that day.' Daniel did not speak, but waited as she went on. 'Papa was hurt a little and I was hurt a lot.'

'Who are these people?'

'Criminals who prey on those who might afford to pay them. Men who see an opportunity in the threatening of others and who with a great amount of force can intimidate without fear of redress.' Robert gave him this answer.

'So you refused their demands?'

'You pay once and you never get free,' Amethyst answered, her eyes daring him to criticise things that he knew nothing about. 'People have been brought in to protect us since, and this was working well until…' She faltered.

'Until I found your father in the alley a few moments away from having the life being beaten out of him?'

Unexpectedly she smiled. 'They were more afraid of you than any man Papa had employed before. It is one of the reasons we offered you the marriage agreement.'

'I see.' Did these people always have to be so wearingly honest in their truths? Daniel's own jaded understanding of principle had long ago been leached from him and there was a sort of brave virtue in such directness. The *ton* would tear such rectitude to pieces, he thought, and wondered how life could mould people so differently.

'Have those demanding money ever contacted you in the form of a letter?'

Robert took over the discourse now. 'Once they did. More normally they just turn up unannounced at the warehouse door.'

'Do you still have the correspondence?'

'Yes.'

'And yet you have not sought anyone to help you in this matter?'

'Help me?' Robert's voice was puzzled.

'Threaten them back. Make them realise they were playing a game they had no hope of ever winning.'

The Earl's tone was weary, Amethyst thought. The utter nuisance of having to deal with people of the trade who had a raft of bullies chasing after them was more than he wanted to consider. Why, he probably thought such inconvenience was par for the course, just another way to show how base and shabby those below him in rank really were.

She wondered if he would simply turn tail and let himself out of this room full of problems, his beautifully cut tailcoat showing off fine shoulders and the breeches long and tapered legs.

A man of reduced means but of great presence, a man whom women would watch with hope in their hearts. Even she had watched him as he had ascended the stairs with her father outside of Tattersall's and dreamed that she was a different girl with softer hair falling to her hips in luxurious waves as he admired her.

Such nonsense made her smile. She was her father's daughter with trade flowing through her less-than-exalted blood line, the hunt of a good deal or an unexpected profit making her life…whole. Women like her did not marry for love and men like Lord Daniel Wylde invariably chose the beautiful butterflies who were the toast of a society Season.

It was only lack of money that stopped him doing exactly that and thinking otherwise would lead to disappointment. The marriage agreement held as much fear for her as it did for him, but she needed her father protected and she wanted to see him face the last months of his life with hope.

She had visited his doctor alone on her own accord after her father had told her of his ailment. The specialist had reiterated that there was little more the medical fraternity could do, but had been most insistent on the medicinal value of hope. Miracles had arisen from a happy demeanour or a looked-forward-to occasion that the sick one had no intentions of missing. Aye, he had said in tones that bridged no argument, there were miracles in the benefits of laughter that even the greatest brains of the time had not yet figured out. 'Keep him happy, Miss Cameron, and he may live longer. That is the only sage advice I can give you at this point.'

Well, Amethyst decided, she would do everything in her power to advance this theory and her papa would have each second of his life tempered with good humour and possibilities. She swore to the heavens above that this would be so.

A few moments later after a general conversation with her father on the merits of a horse that had won a recent race at Newmarket, Lord Montcliffe reached for his hat and made for the door, giving only the briefest of goodbyes to her as he left. A man who was being forced into something he plainly did not want and yet, given his circumstances, could not refuse.

They were so much the same, Amethyst

thought, as the door shut behind him and the hollow silence that was left only underlined the awful truth of her musing.

Chapter Four

Daniel sat in his library that evening before a fire that was both warm and comforting. Looking up, he frowned at the portrait of his brother lording it over the room. He would have a servant take the painting down on the morrow and he would find a landscape of Spain he knew to be somewhere in the confines of this town house. Nigel's foolishness had brought the Earldom to this pass and he wanted no more of a reminder of his brother's handsome visage smiling down upon his own dire straits.

The cool of early evening moved in about him despite the fire flame in the hearth, his leg still aching with the slightest of movements. Outside a dog called, the plaintive howl answered as he listened and silently counted the hours until the dawn. How often had he sat like this since his return from Europe? Even as he massaged the tight knots in his thigh, others formed in their place, iron-hard against the skin that covered muscle. His leg was getting worse. He knew it was. Would there come a day when he could not bear weight upon it at all? He swore beneath his breath and resolved not to think about it.

A knock at his door had him returning his leg to the floor and when his man came in with a card showing that Miss Amethyst Cameron was waiting to see him, his eyes glanced at the clock. Half past eight. My God. No time at all for a young and single woman of any station in life to be calling upon a gentleman without the repercussion of ruin. Following his servant to the lobby he found his bride-to-be standing there, no lady's maid at her side and no papa to keep everything above board and proper, either. Glancing around, he was relieved to see a Cameron footman waiting in the shadow of the porch, ready to shepherd her back through the evening.

'I am very sorry to come at such a late hour, but I need to speak with you, my lord.'

Worry marred her brow and she seemed relieved as he gestured her through to the blue salon, the scent of lemon and flowers following her in. Her dull brown hair this evening was pulled back and fastened with a glittery pin. It was the first piece of jewellery he had ever seen her wear.

'Carole, one of the little girls at Gaskell Street, made the fastener for me and presented it to me this evening,' she explained when she realised what had caught his attention. 'A beaker was broken at the school last week and she fashioned the shards of china into a clip.' Her smile broadened and it had the effect of making her eyes look bigger in her face than they usually were. And much more gold. Perfectly arched dark eyebrows sat above them.

'I have just come from the school concert, my lord.' Even as she said it she removed the clip from her hair and deposited it in a large cloth bag she carried.

'You work there?'

'No, I am a patron, my lord, a small recompense for all that they did for me as a child. We are building a new dormitory that will be ready in a matter of only a few weeks and there is much yet to finish and so—' She stopped abruptly and blushed. 'But you cannot possibly be interested in any of this. Papa said I should only speak of happy things, light topics and suchlike. Orphans and all of their accompanying poverty, I suppose, do not come into that category.'

He had to smile. 'I hope I am not quite so shallow, Miss Cameron. The work sounds useful and interesting.'

'Then you would not stop me being involved? You would allow me the independence that I need after this marriage?'

When he nodded Daniel had the sudden impression that he might have been agreeing to far more than he knew he was, but she soon went on to another topic altogether.

'Papa's insistence on a harmonious union should not be too onerous either, my lord. Nowhere in the marriage document is there any mention of how many days a year we would need to reside together. It need not be a trap.'

'Are you always this forthright, Miss Cameron?'

'Yes.' No qualification. She looked at him as if he had just given her the biggest compliment in the world.

'Clinical.'

'Pragmatic,' she returned and blushed to almost the same shade as a scarlet rug thrown across a nearby sofa.

Such vulnerability lurking amongst brave endeavour was strangely endearing and although he meant not to Daniel caught at her hand. He wanted to protect her from a world that would not quite know what to make of her; his world, where the cut of a cloth was as important as the name of the family and the consideration of others less fortunate in means was best left to the worry of others or to nobody at all.

As he had already noted, she smelt of lemon and flowers, none of the heady heavy aromas the ladies in court seemed to be drawn towards and desire ignited within him, as unexpected as it was unwanted. Abruptly he let her go.

'You must know that it is not done for a lady to visit a gentleman alone, Miss Cameron, under any circumstances.'

'Oh, I am not a lady, my lord.'

'You soon will be.'

Again she shook her head. 'I do not wish to change, Lord Montcliffe. There is just simply too much for me to do. This is why I have come to make certain that you know…' She stopped, and he got the impression she was trying to work out exactly how she might give him her truths.

'Know what?'

'I will marry you, my lord, and my father will in turn nullify the debts of your family. But in exchange I wish for two things.'

She waited as he nodded.

'I want you to make certain no one will ever bother my father again and I want you to promise that when Papa leaves this world…' her voice caught '…you will let me go.'

'Let you go?'

'I will not contest the monies at all, though I will expect a substantial settlement and Dunstan House, of course, and its accompanying lands.'

'My God. You are serious?'

She nodded her head. 'I am a business woman, my lord, and astute enough to know that this marriage is only one of convenience. You would never have chosen me without the enticement of great wealth and I accept that, but I do want civility and fairness.'

Each word she said was more astonishing than the last. He had had all manner of women throwing themselves at him for years and here was one telling him to his face that a marriage between them was purely a matter of business, and finite at that.

'What of your needs in this union, Miss Cameron?'

'I don't have any as such, Lord Montcliffe. I simply want my father to be content in the last months of his life. That is all.'

Daniel was not one to turn away from such a gauntlet.

'And emotion? Where does that fit into this conundrum?'

She shook her head vigorously, the brown tresses marked with no sheen from the lamp-light. She had stepped back too, her strange large bag positioned between them like a barrier.

'I do realise that as a titled gentleman you would require the production of heirs and as such this agreement will give you the time to find a woman you would want as the chosen mother of your children. You are not so old, after all, and gentlemen of the *ton* have a marked propensity to choose much younger wives from what I have observed.'

Without meaning to he smiled, such direct honesty so very unfamiliar.

His glance went to her lips, full and defined,

and he felt a surge of desire. God, it had been years since his libido had been so fickle and months since he had last bedded a woman.

The world seemed to stand still between them, any logic sucked into pure and utter confusion. Any other female of his acquaintance would have simpered and flushed in such a situation, but she stood there watching him, her glance strong and unwavering.

'I also hope you are of the same opinion concerning this marriage as I am and share the belief that it would require no...no...' She stopped, searching around for what to say and failing.

'Intimacy?' He gave the word in humour, but she paled visibly, reminding him in that moment of a skittish colt, wanting to be reassured on the one hand and ready to bolt on the other.

'I realise, my lord, that there must be a great many young women in the *ton* who would jump at the chance of being an earl's wife in general and your wife in particular. Even with the imminent financial collapse of the Montcliffe estate I feel certain you would still be a good catch. With the Cameron fortune behind you there would be a far better chance of acquiring exactly the sort of woman you would wish for. I could simply disappear and never be seen again, a former spouse who should not be a problem if I was to be thought of as dead. I would be quite happy with such an outcome if Papa was no longer with me. Indeed, I could go to the Continent and settle under a different name.'

'You are seriously expounding bigamy?'

He began to laugh then, because what she said was becoming more and more outlandish and because he could barely believe that she was saying it.

'Perhaps I am, my lord, though in the very best sense of the word, of course, and mutually agreed. I would also like to add that I wouldn't have acquiesced to a union between us if I had not liked your character. I realised, quite early on, that it was most unlikely you would have ever been attracted to me in the slightest, had we met under other circumstances, and there was a good deal of safety in that.'

A challenge thrown down between them, Daniel thought to himself, and given with such an engaging and disarming frankness.

'Such safety, Miss Cameron, is not the best building block for any marriage and I shall show you exactly why.' Without asking for permission, he dispensed with the bag and brought her into his arms.

She should have been horrified. She should have fought off his grip and demanded release as his hands brought her in and his lips came down on hers. But her head would not obey her heart as warmth seared into disbelief and the world narrowed to a feeling that began in a place low in her stomach, before exploding everywhere.

His kiss was not gentle or tentative or kind. It was raw and masculine with an edge of anger demanding response. It was deep and unexpected, his tongue finding hers as the angle of the kiss changed, slanting on to another plane, splayed palms guiding her in, the sound of breath, the dissolution of the world around them, the focus of heat and want and need.

Another language that she had had no notion of. The clock in the corner with its heavy beat seemed to stop as she tasted him in return, his strength, his toughness, the sheer and potent force of a man who understood the power he wielded. There was no question of resisting. When her nails traced a runnel in his skin to bring him closer, his lips slid down the sensitive line of her neck. They would mark each other with this moment, she thought, as she tipped her head, the column of her throat exposed to the hard pull of his mouth.

But as his hand wandered to trace the line of her bottom under her billowing skirt she jerked back, the hue on her cheeks rising. This was unlike anything she had imagined. The danger of her response made her feel dizzy.

She needed to be gone, away from this room, away from the things that she knew must be reflected in her eyes and on her face and in the hard twin buds of desire that pushed against the material in her bodice.

She was pleased both for the coat and for the fact that he had turned to face the window so that she did not need to see his expression. Not yet. With shaking hands she opened the door.

'I am glad we had this…t-talk, my lord, but now I must go.'

Then she was outside, her footman following closely behind down the steps of the Montcliffe town house. As they gained the road the servant gestured to the Cameron conveyance a good hundred yards away to collect them. She had asked the driver to park there, away from the prying eyes of others.

She prayed Daniel Wylde would not follow to demand an answer to all that had transpired between them. Her father was dying and she would do anything at all in her power to make him happy, even marry a man who, she knew in that very second, could only break her heart. Wiping away a tear, she swallowed and took a deep breath, the strength she had always kept a hold on returning.

At least he understood now the parameters of this relationship. Or did he?

'Hell.' Daniel adjusted the fit of his trousers over a growing hardness. She had dumbfounded him with her reaction to his kiss, no tepid chaste reply, but a full-blown taking of everything he had offered, the promise of lust in the way her teeth had come down on his bottom lip, egging on all that he had held restrained.

Like a siren. Like a courtesan. Like a woman of far more experience than she was admitting to.

His plain little intended mouse-to-be was baring her claws and turning into a lioness and all before they had even got up the matrimonial aisle. Nothing made sense any more because the only thing he was thinking about was following her and demanding the completion of an intimacy that had left him reeling.

He was glad that her scent lingered in the room, glad to keep the promise of Amethyst Cameron for a little while longer. The cloth bag she had brought in was still beside the sofa, abandoned in her moment of panic, some item of clothing spilling out on to his thick burgundy Aubusson carpet.

As he hauled the thing upwards, one handle broke and the contents tumbled out. An apron and a tattered Bible were the first things that had fallen at his feet, Amethyst's name printed in the frontispiece of the book and underlined in different colours. He smiled, imagining her doing such a thing. Beneath that was a ragdoll with a torn dress and another toy whose identity he could not determine—a cat perhaps, its paws missing. Incredibly, a diamond ring also sat there amongst the folds of cloth, the carat weight sizeable, and the cut, colour and clarity unmatched. Valuable and forgotten, strands of cotton and dust caught in the clasps of gold.

Any other woman of his acquaintance would have worn the thing on her finger, showing it off, enjoying the admiration of others, but not Amethyst Cameron. No, to her the dismembered cat probably had more of a value and the Bible a better use.

Stuffing the lot back in the bag, he called to his footman.

'Have this delivered to the Camerons' home in Grosvenor Square immediately.' Daniel did not wish to take the thing himself, an unaccustomed fragility setting his countenance on edge after the last few minutes with his bride-to-be.

He tried not to notice the curiosity in his man's eyes as he handed the bag over.

Her father was still up when she got home and Amethyst's heart sank. Of all the nights he had delayed retiring to his bedchamber, why did it have to be this one?

'Papa.' She tried to keep her voice steady, but knew that she had not succeeded as he stood.

'What has happened? You look...different.'

She almost smiled at that. *Different.* Such a word came nowhere near the heart of all that she felt.

'I went to see Lord Montcliffe.'

'And?'

'I am not certain if he was the right choice after all. I think he might want a lot from me, more than I should be willing to give.'

Her father laughed. 'Your mother said that of me.'

'He kissed me.'

The stillness in his eyes was foreign. 'Did you like it?'

Her heart thudded as she nodded.

'Then he was the right choice, Amy, for although society is disparaging in allowing any intimate contact between intending couples I think that it should be mandatory. As long as it is a consenting thing. He did not force you?'

'No.'

'If your mother was here, she would tell you of the power of feelings between a man and a woman and she would say it better than I. Whitely knew nothing about you, my dear. He did not appreciate the layers in a woman or the complexities.'

Anger rose where only guilt had lingered. Until this moment Amethyst had always thought their broken marriage was her fault, but after Daniel Wylde's kiss she wondered. Gerald had kissed her a few times in the very early days of their courtship, but his pecks were tepid reflections of all she had felt in the heated atmosphere of Lord Montcliffe's library. The breath constricted in her throat and she swallowed back worry. If she could react this way to one of the Earl's kisses, what might happen if things went further? The teachers at Gaskell Street had always drilled her upon the proper and correct reactions a lady might show to the world and she was certain that her response tonight would have been well outside any appropriate boundary.

Decorum and seemliness were the building stones of the aristocracy. The gentler sex was supposed to be exactly that, after all—women devoid of all the more natural vices men were renowned for. She wished her mother was here to give some advice and direction. Her father, however, seemed, more than ready to supply some.

'Whitely was a conniving liar, that was the problem. He was no more than an acquaintance when you married him and nothing more when he died. I tried to warn you, but you would not listen. If your mother had still been alive, I am certain things would have been different, but it is hard to advise anyone against something they have their very heart set upon.'

His words dug into Amethyst's centre. Her fault. Her mistake. Her deficiency to tumble into a relationship that had been patently wrong from the very start.

With Gerald there had been no true underpinning attraction. With Daniel it was the opposite. She did not know him at all and yet… She shook away the justification. Lust was shaky ground to build a relationship upon and she could not afford another disaster.

Her father's coughing started in a little way at first, a clearing of a throat, a slight impediment. But then his eyes rolled back and he simply dropped, folding in on himself, a slight man with his jacket askew and his spectacles crushed underfoot.

She shouted out as the doorbell rang and the Cameron butler and a stranger rushed into the room, the bag she had left at the Montcliffe town house abandoned at their feet as they both lifted her father to the *chaise longue*. Wilson untied his cravat and loosened his collar, arranging Robert on his side so that his breathing was eased.

Amethyst could not move. She was frozen in fear as the numbness spreading across her chest emptied her of rational thought. Was it his heart? Was this the final moment of which the specialist had spoken?

'Get a doctor.' Their butler seemed to have taken charge and the man she did not know nodded and left the room. A Montcliffe servant, she supposed, returning her bag. Nothing made sense any more. The housekeeper scurried in with a hot towel and a bowl, the maid kneeling with new wood to stoke up the heat of the fire, Wilson trying to awaken her father from the stupor he had fallen into. The moments turned into a good half an hour.

And then Lord Montcliffe was there, his voice calm with authority as he took in the situation, a doctor at his side.

Amethyst's jaw ached from where she held it tightly together, but when he took her arm and led her across to her father, she went.

'Hold his hand and sit beside him. Talk to him so that he knows you are there.'

When Robert's wilted fingers came into her grasp she held on. Cold. Familiar. The scar upon his little finger where he had fallen through glass, a nail pulled out by heavy timber. A working man's hand and the hand of a father who had loved her well. She brought the back of it to her lips, paper-thin skin marred by brown spots, age drawn into years of outside work. Kissing him, she willed him back, willed him to open his eyes and see her. The doctor frowned as he felt for a pulse.

'Is there other family we can call?'

She shook her head.

Just her and just Papa. The horror of loss ran through her like sharpened swords and her teeth had begun to chatter, shock searing into trauma. For a moment the next breath just would not come.

Daniel kneeled down before her, hoping the panic he could see in her eyes might allow her more of an ease of breath. 'Anything that can be done for your father will be, Miss Cameron. MacKenzie, my physician, is the best doctor there is in London. Do you understand?'

Her eyes focused upon him, a tiny flare of hope scrambling over alarm.

'Already with the blankets and the fire he is becoming warmer and the blueness is leaving his lips.'

This time she nodded her head, one slow tear leaking from her left eye and tracing its way down her cheek.

Both of the Camerons looked as pale as the other and as thin. He had not noticed her thinness until this moment, when devoid of her coat in the bright light he could see her arms and her collarbones and the meagreness of her waist.

She did not court fashion, that much was certain. Her boots were sturdy leather and well worn, as though they had covered many a mile, and still had some life left in them. But sitting there in the grip of tragedy, there was a fineness about Amethyst Cameron that was mesmerising. All he wanted to do was to hold her away from the hurt and make things better. To protect her against a world that was often cruel, complex and dishonest. To shield her from pain, duplicity and scorn.

When the doctor gestured him over he stood.

'Mr Cameron will need to be watched, my lord, but I think we have passed the worst of it. All his vital signs are settling and I should well imagine that he will recover from this turn.'

Daniel knew Amethyst had heard the given words even though she was a good distance away. He also knew that if he stayed in the house without a chaperone for any longer then tongues would begin to wag. It was late after all.

'I will leave the doctor with you then, Miss Cameron, and hope your father has a good night.' He met her eyes only briefly and her countenance was one of worry, no glimpse at all alluding to the kiss they had shared less than an hour earlier. He was pleased for it.

'I appreciate your help, Lord Montcliffe.'

So formal and distant, he thought, as she escorted him to the front lobby, one of the servants finding his coat and hat. Her hair looked odd too, the front of it hitched askew in a strange fashion. Nothing about this woman seemed to make sense to him and he was relieved to slip through the door and into the coolness of the night air.

Leaning against the portal and closing her eyes for just a moment Amethyst listened to the Montcliffe carriage pull away. 'One second, two seconds, three seconds,' she counted, holding the world back from all that was crashing in upon her. Her mama had taught her this years before, a small space of time in which to collect one's thoughts or feelings. The feeling of Daniel Wylde's kiss snaked into her consciousness even as she tried to shut it out.

When at length she gathered herself, Amethyst caught her reflection in a mirror opposite and horror and laughter mingled on her face in equal measure.

Her wig had been snagged at some point and was sitting at an angle on her head, the right side dragging the left down and giving her an appearance of someone out of sorts with the world.

With care she readjusted the hairpiece. Had this just happened or had Lord Montcliffe seen it as well? The whole evening had been tumultuous; her father's strange malady counterbalanced against the Earl of Montcliffe's unexpected kiss.

Wiping her forefinger along the lines of her lips, she then held it still, the impression of flesh sending small shards of want into a sense that had long been dormant.

She was known for her composure and her unruffled calm. She seldom let things bother her and always managed people with acumen and honesty.

Unflappable Amethyst. Until Lord Daniel Wylde.

He made her think of possibilities that would not come to pass. She was ruined goods and she was plain. Without the Montcliffe financial problems and the collection by her father of the extensive Goldsmith debts, he would never have given her a second glance.

She could not allow herself to be one of those pathetic women who didn't see the truth of their loveless marriages and held on for year after year for something that was impossible.

Two years was what she could give him. Two years in which her father would not be sad or worried or unhappy. If he even lived that long, which was doubtful.

The Earl of Montcliffe would not love her and she would not let herself love him. But together they could manage. The kiss had thrown her, that was all, an unexpected chink in the armour she had long pulled about her.

Liar. Liar. Liar. The words ran together as a refrain as she hurried back to her father.

Lucien Howard, Earl of Ross, sat beside Daniel in the card room of White's an hour later. Smoke swirled around in curls and the smell of strong liquor filled any space left as some patrons won a little and others lost a lot.

'I hear you bought those remarkable Arabian greys at Tattersall's?' There was a good measure of curiosity in his friend's query.

'You know enough about my present circumstances, Luce, to know I could never afford them.'

'Then why are they in your care?'

'Have you heard of the trader, Mr Robert Cameron?'

'No. Who is he?'

'A man who sells timber to the world.'

'Lucrative, then?'

'Very. He wants me to marry his daughter.'

Brandy slopped against the side of the glass as Lucien lurched forward. 'You agreed?'

'The matching pair of greys came as a sweetener. Montcliffe Manor is bankrupt and it will only be a matter of months before the rest of the world knows the fact.' He raised his glass and then swallowed a good part of the contents of the bottle he had ordered. 'If I do nothing, it will all be gone.'

Lucien was quiet for a moment, but then he smiled. 'What does the daughter look like?'

'Passable.'

'Your bastard of a father must be laughing in the afterlife then. At least he was a man of his word. I remember him insisting that you wouldn't inherit a farthing of his fortune and he meant it.'

'The curse of the Wyldes?' Daniel's thoughts fell into words.

'How long do you have left, do you think, if you sat it out and did nothing?'

'It will only be a matter of weeks before the first creditors arrive.' Leaning back against soft leather, he ran his hands through his hair. 'I have had word that they are already circling.'

'I'd lend you money if I had any, but my situation is about as dire as your own.'

'Your grandfather wants to disinherit your side of the family again? I heard about it from Francis before he left for Bath.'

'Where he has gone to try to sort out his own financial woes, no doubt. Seems he has a cousin a few times removed there causing him some trouble.'

Daniel smiled. 'The three of us have our problems then, though mine could be solved before the month is up.'

'You will go through with it? This betrothal?'

'Marriage or bankruptcy? I have little choice.'

'It wasn't supposed to be like this. We were all going to travel to the Far East and make our fortunes, remember? God, that sort of innocence seems so long ago.'

'The naivety of youth.'

'Or the hope of it. Marriage is a big step, Daniel. Is this bride-to-be at least intelligent?'

'Undeniably.'

'Does she simper?'

'No.'

'An heiress who has brains and is not prone to whining? Perhaps you have made more of a match than you imagine. What colour is her hair?'

'A dull mouse.'

Lucien began to laugh. 'And her eyes?'

'Brown.'

'Is she fat?'

'Thin.'

'Short?'

'No.'

'Mama was always certain you would marry the moody but beautiful Charlotte Hughes. She is back, you know, from Scotland and without the husband.'

'Spenser Mackay died by all accounts.'

'But in doing so he left her a fortune which she probably needs about as much as you do. The *ton* likes to think you were heartbroken when she left, Daniel.'

'A good tale is often more interesting than a truthful one.'

'Have you told the Countess about your upcoming nuptials?'

'I haven't.'

'But you will?'

'No. The wedding is in a few weeks' time. Mother would need at least a month to get ready for it and even that might not be enough. Would you be the best man, Luce?'

'I would be honoured to.'

'Francis will be the usher, I hope. I sent a message to Bath yesterday telling him of the plans. The announcement will be in *The Times* next week.'

'A few more hours of peace, then. When can I meet your intended?'

'I'm calling on her on Monday. Perhaps you might accompany me?'

A furore at the other end of the room caught their attention and Lord Gabriel Hughes, the fourth Earl of Wesley, strode in, a tall stranger hanging on his shoulder and pushed off with a nonchalance that was surprising.

'London is not as it was, my lords. Nordmeyer insists that I insulted his sister and wants to call me out for it.'

'And did you insult her?'

'She sent me a note arranging a meeting and he found it. I hardly think that was my fault.'

'But you would have met her if the letter had arrived?'

'Undoubtedly.'

Laughter was as good a medicine as any, Daniel thought as Gabe ordered a drink. A few years ago he and Gabriel Hughes had been good friends, but he hadn't seen much of him lately. Charlotte's influence, perhaps. The women in the family had always been surprisingly persuasive.

'I hear you were the one who bought the pair of greys showing at Tattersall's a few weeks back, Montcliffe. Richard Tattersall had designs to procure them himself, but it seems you beat him to it with an irrefusable offer.'

Daniel wondered where this story had originated. Robert Cameron, perhaps, for the man was as wily as he was rich.

'The Montcliffe coffers must be in good shape, then, for they would have not come cheap,' Gabriel remarked. An undercurrent of question lay in the words. 'And speaking of good shape, my sister is home again and had hoped that you might call upon her?'

'I saw her today. In Regent Street.'

'How did she appear to you?' The heavy frown on Gabriel's forehead was worrying.

'In good health. Your mother was with her.'

'She seldom allows Charlotte out of her sight. I think she is worried that grief might get the better of her.'

'Grief for the death of her husband?'

The short bark of laughter was disconcerting. 'She realised that Spenser Mackay was a mistake before she had even come within a cooee of the Borderlands.'

'Another man, then?' Lucien joined in the conversation now.

But as if realising he had said too much, Gabriel Hughes gestured to the waiter and ordered another drink.

'I propose a toast to our bachelorhood, gentlemen, and long may it last.' As Lucien lifted his glass Daniel caught his eyes and the deep humour obvious in the blue depths was disconcerting.

Chapter Five

Daniel Wylde and she were in bed at Dunstan House, candlelight covering their bodies and her hair to the waist.

'Love me for ever, my beautiful Amethyst,' he said as he brought his lips down upon her own, hard and slanted, desire moulding her body into his, asking for all that she knew he would give her. His fingers framed her face, tilting her into the caress, building the connection. 'Love me as I love you, my darling, never let us be apart.'

And then she was awake in her own chamber at Grosvenor Square, the moon high outside. Alone. The dream of Lord Montcliffe dissolved into a formless want and the need that she had no hope in wishing for dissipated. He would not love her like that, he could not.

Pushing back the covers, she stood and lit a candle before crossing to the bookshelves on one side of the room.

Here behind a row of burgundy leather tomes she found what she had hidden. Her diary. A narrative of Gerald Whitely and their time together, every emotion she had felt for him penned in black and white. And in red, too, her blood smeared across one page mixed in troth with his. A small cut below the nail of her thumb. Sometimes she felt it with the pad of her opposing finger. He had laughed at the time and told her she was being melodramatic. Then he had stopped laughing altogether. The small book fell open at one of the pages.

I hate him. I hate everything about him. I hate his drunkenness and his anger. I hate it that I was stupid enough to become his wife. I think Papa suspects that there is something wrong between us and I hate that, too.

As she riffled through to the end of the book, there seemed to be a myriad of variations on that theme and she remembered again exactly what hopelessness felt like.

After his death she had not trusted anyone

except for her father. After Gerald the world of possibility and expectation had shrunk into a formless mist, her big mistake relegated to that part of her mind which refused to be hurt again, but even thirteen months later the horror had left an indelible mark.

The business of making money had been healing, saving her from the ignominy of venturing back into the pursuit of another mate. Oh, she had gone to Gerald's funeral and attended his grave, placing flowers and small offerings because it was expected. She had also worn her mourning garb for the obligatory year because she could have not borne the questions that might have occurred otherwise. Even in death she had not betrayed him.

A single tear dropped upon the sheet below, blurring the careful writing.

A blemished bride. Then and now. Granted, she came to this next union with a dowry that was substantial and with the means to save a family on the brink of devastation. It must count for something.

But the kiss Daniel Wylde and she had shared was worrying because in it were the seeds of her own destruction.

Not like Gerald Whitely. Not like him at all.

The voyeur inside her who had been watching others for years was threatened, the safe distance she had fostered shattered by a hope she had never known, for when Lord Montcliffe had taken her hand and then her lips something in her had risen and his gold-green eyes had known it had.

Looking back, she could not understand just what had led her into the mistake of marrying Whitely in the first place. Loneliness, perhaps, or the fact that the years were rushing by. Certainly it had not been a blinding love or even a distilled version of affection. No, she had married Gerald because no one else had ever given her a second look and she was starting to feel as if spinsterhood was just around a very close corner.

Her father's respect for his business acumen might have also made a difference. Amythest wanted to marry a man whom Robert would regard with fondness and Gerald had arrived at the warehouse with glowing references and a comforting confidence. A man who at first brought her flowers and pretty handkerchiefs and professed that he had never in his whole life seen anyone as beautiful as she was.

When the nasty side of him had surfaced a

month or so before their marriage she should have cut her losses and run. Her father would have understood and there was no one else whose opinion she cared much about. Yet still she had persisted in believing that she could calm Gerald's anger and gently soothe all the problems he seemed to have with others.

Marriage had changed that. The admonishments had been verbal at first, just small criticisms of her dress and her hair. Then he had used his fists.

Fear had held her rigid and distant, the shame and the anger at her stupidity buried under a carefully constructed outer mask. She could not believe that she had been so gullible and foolish as to imagine a wonderful life with a man she had barely known. When he had died sixteen months later Amethyst had not seen him for a good handful of weeks before that and her heartfelt relief added to the guilt of everything.

Four mornings after the kiss she had shared with Lord Montcliffe she felt full of anxiety. Her intended was waiting downstairs in the Blue Salon and he had brought a friend with him. To see what trap the Earl had tumbled into, she supposed, the sour taste of trade balanced by a wife who was at least wealthy enough to save Montcliffe.

After nights of poor sleep and lurid dreams Amethyst felt exposed; pinned to a board like a butterfly in some scientific laboratory, wings outstretched and colours fading into dust. No possible defences. No protection against the disdain he surely must be feeling.

At least the wig felt like armour and the dark purple bombazine in her gown was sturdy enough to withstand any amount of derision. As she opened the door of the salon they had been directed to, the smile on her face was tight.

'My lord.' She did not allow Daniel Wylde to take her fingers or to touch her as she inclined her head.

'Miss Cameron.' There was a slight hesitation in his greeting. 'I hope your father has had a few comfortable nights and is feeling better after his fall.'

'He is, my lord, thank you, though he is under strict instructions to stay in bed for a few more days yet. Your doctor was most insistent about that. Perhaps I should have informed you,' she added as an afterthought, suddenly uncertain of the rules around being unchaperoned even in her own house.

'We will not stay long. May I introduce my good friend to you? Lucien Howard, Earl of Ross, this is Miss Amethyst Amelia Cameron, my intended.'

The man who stood by the mantelpiece watched her carefully. With hair as pale as Daniel Wylde's was dark, he held the same sort of stillness and menace. She also thought she saw a hitch of puzzlement in his eyes.

'Montcliffe has told me all about you, Miss Cameron.'

'I should not think there would be much to say, my lord.'

Unexpectedly Lord Ross laughed. 'Actually, I am more surprised by all he didn't.'

Glancing over at Daniel, Amethyst wondered how much honesty he would allow. She decided to test him.

'It is a truism that great wealth holds a loud persuasion. As a good friend of Montcliffe's you must realise this.'

The stance of relaxed grace did not change a whit, but Lord Montcliffe had moved closer and Amethyst felt that same sharp jolt of shock with an ache. She did not look her best today, she knew it. The wig itched unremittingly and the red around her eyes from poor sleep did her no favours whatsoever. She had tried to assuage the damage with some powder she had asked her maid to fetch from the pharmacist yesterday, but the application was difficult and she wondered if instead of hiding the problem she had accentuated it. She wished now that she had simply wiped the powder off before entering the room.

'Miss Cameron runs the books for the Cameron timber company, Luce. According to her father she is irreplaceable in her knowledge of the trade.'

Was the Earl criticising her? His words did not seem slanted with distaste so mayhap this was another example of her not comprehending the ways of the *ton*. His friend's face was carefully schooled to show as little emotion as Montcliffe's did, allowing her no way of understanding the truth.

'I have heard it said that you have a knowledge of horseflesh too, Miss Cameron? Your father's pair of greys were the talk of the town a few weeks back and, when I went in to look them over, Tattersall mentioned your name on the ownership deeds.'

'Papa and I generally consult on new purchases, my lord. That particular pair was procured on a trip we made to Spain together three years ago.' She stopped, thinking perhaps she sounded boastful.

'I see. Montcliffe raised horses when we were younger too. Before the war took us into Spain and they were lost to him.'

'You were in the army, as well?'

'It is the curse of an estate of great title, but little in the way to support it, Miss Cameron. 'Twas either that or the church and the stipend in religion is miserable.'

As he said the words Lucien Howard turned and the light from the window directly behind him fell across a large swathe of scarring at his neck. Averting her eyes, Amethyst hoped he had not seen just where her interest lay, though when she glanced over at Daniel she knew a momentary consternation. The easy-going lord of the realm seemed replaced by another, hard distance coating his every feature, memory overlaid by anger.

War wounds. She had seen the soldiers from the Peninsular Campaign as they had stumbled up the quayside of all the ports between Falmouth and Dover the previous year in the final days of January. She had been in the south with her father, checking on a new timber delivery, and the filthy, ill and skeletal men had been a shocking sight. Thirty-five thousand men had crossed the Spanish frontier to march against Napoleon and eight thousand had not returned. Lord Montcliffe and his friend Lord Ross had no doubt been amongst those on the crowded transports in the Bay of Biscay storms. She could barely imagine what nightmares such a journey would have brought.

Daniel was a stranger to her, all the pieces of his past unknown and the sum of his whole unchartered. The cold thought clawed into consciousness but she shook such a musing away, colouring as she realised her guests were looking at her as though expecting an answer to a question.

'I am sorry, I did not hear what you asked.'

'Lucien wished to know if you would allow his younger sister to help you get ready on your wedding day.'

'Oh.' Amethyst did not quite know how to answer this. She had always been surrounded by men in the business of trading timber and had seldom had the time to foster any relationship with women.

The Earl of Ross took up the conversation now. 'Christine lost her betrothed in the march up to La Corunna and she is a little depressed. Helping in the preparation for a wedding might be just the distraction she needs.'

'I should imagine your sister would find me most dull.'

'She loves hairstyles and dresses and decorating homes.'

Amethyst's heart sank.

'And she can make an occasion of anything.'

Hard to make an occasion with the two participants pressed into a union neither wished for. Placing a false smile on her lips, Amethyst nodded.

'Then I would be most thankful for her help.'

Montcliffe appeared as though he was about to laugh, but the arrival of the maid with an assortment of small cakes and lemonade put paid to that expression. Pouring three generous glasses, she handed one to each of them and invited them to sit down.

'The speciality of the house is this lemon syrup. I hope you will enjoy it.' The lemonade was cold and sour, exactly the way she and her father liked it, yet both men looked to be struggling with the taste. Even yesterday she might have been mortified to think that the beverage was not quite right, but today for some reason the fact made her smile.

The control she seldom lost hold of had seemed to slip of late and the small victory was welcomed. She knew, of course, that they would be far more at home with some alcoholic drink, but it was only just midday and the hour seemed too early to be serving something as strong without Papa present.

When Lord Montcliffe stood she was certain that he would be taking his leave, but he walked across to the window instead to observe a view of the park opposite.

'This house is well situated. Do you take exercise there?'

'Sometimes I do, my lord. More normally though I ride my horse in Hyde Park in the late afternoon.'

'Will you be there tomorrow?'

He had not turned, but she felt a palpable tension as he waited for her answer.

'I shall. I take a turn or two around Rotten Row most days.'

'Good.'

At that Lucien Howard also stood and both men gave their leave and were gone within a moment. When the door shut behind them Amethyst remained very still. Had Daniel arranged a meeting between them for tomorrow or not? The two almost-full glasses of lemonade stood on the table and she picked up the one Daniel had used and sipped from it. Ridiculous, she knew, but he made her feel that way: girlish, breathless, terrified.

Her father's bell was ringing. Papa was waiting for an account of the meeting, she supposed, but still she did not move. Would Daniel ride alone tomorrow? Her maid always accompanied her to the park, but stayed on a seat near the gateway. Would this allow them some privacy? Did she want it?

Gerald had been disappointed in her so very quickly. She had held his attention only briefly before he had ventured forth to find other avenues of satisfaction. He had found her gauche and stiff. He had told her that the night he had left for the last time, a wife who was nothing like he had imagined she would be, but she could not dwell on it. 'I deserve to be happy, and so does Papa,' she muttered to herself and caught sight of a small bird on a branch outside.

'If I close my eyes and count to ten and it is still there, then all shall be fine.'

When she opened them the sight of an empty

branch greeted her, the buds of new leaves shivering with the motion of its parting.

Signs. She looked for them everywhere now, good and bad, but the hectic tinkle of her father's bell had her moving from the room and up the wide oaken staircase.

She absolutely had to tell him. Today. Now. This minute. The early evening light sending redness into his raven hair and the green of the oaks all about them.

I have been married before. My husband died in a brothel because he could no longer abide the pretence of me in his marriage bed. It was not a successful union and by the end of it we hated each other.

That was what she should have said. Out loud. With conviction. Let Daniel run before the knots tied them irrevocably together and the blame game began. But she stayed silent as she watched him rein in his steed and move beside her. The time to confess everything about her tawdry past was not quite right and she wanted just for this moment to enjoy his company. Next time. She would definitely tell him of her unfortunate mistake next time they met.

'I did not think you were coming,' he remarked.

'Papa passed a fidgety night and I have spent the day reading to him as it makes him relax. I was not certain you would wait.'

'Then we both have much to learn about the other, Miss Cameron, for I have the patience of a saint.'

He didn't look like anything celestial with his wild black hair caught in an untidy queue and his snowy cravat highlighting the darkness of his skin. Nay, today atop the power of his steed he looked like a soldier who might rule the world and use it in whatever way he wished.

The wickedness of his smile and the dancing pale green in his eyes took her form in, a scorching languid perusal that made her glance away. If she had been braver, she might have laughed into the sudden breeze and used his words as a challenge. She might have even thrown back her own. But the days of her certainty had long gone and the battered ends of the mouse-brown wig flew against her face, making her eyes water.

This is me now, this person, small and damaged and scared. A man like this is not to be played with, not to be taken lightly. The weight of the Cameron fortune was heavy on her shoulders and her father's sickness heavier again as she stayed silent.

'Our marriage notice will be in the paper tomorrow morning. I just thought to warn you of it.'

'Warn me?' She could not quite understand his meaning.

'Society has the habit of being ingratiatingly interested in those who gain a title.'

'Unexpectedly, you mean?'

'A new countess is everybody's business, Miss Cameron. It is the way of the world.'

His focus suddenly centred on a small group of mounted women on the path, the stillness in him magnified as he muttered something under his breath.

'It is probably prudent to say nothing of our upcoming nuptials at this stage.' He stopped his horse and waited and she did the same. 'The *ton* is a small group, but their propensity to gossip is enormous and one wrong word can set them into a frenzy.'

Lady Charlotte Mackay and Lady Astoria Jordan were exactly the pair Daniel had no inclination to meet. Dressed in the finest of riding attire, they looked the picture of well-heeled perfection as they slowed down to chat. Amethyst, on the other hand, seemed to have drawn into herself, lips pursed and eyes dull. The light on her hair did nothing to help her appearance either. For the first time since he had met her he wondered if she wore a wig, ill fashioned and dreary. The thought was surprising.

Charlotte's beauty, on the other hand, seemed to radiate around her, the soft blond of her *coiffure* under the riding cap catching the light and falling in an unbroken line to her ample bosom. A tinkling laugh completed the picture.

'Daniel. I knew it was you.' His name curled from her tongue as an invitation, the intimacy that they had once shared drawn into the words. Her glance took in the woman he was with and his bride-to-be stilled perceptibly.

'Lady Charlotte Mackay, this is Miss Amethyst Cameron.'

'Amethyst. An unusual name, I think.' A frown marred the space between Charlotte's sky-blue eyes as she tried to place the family. 'Are you of the Camerons from Fife in Scotland or those closer?'

'Neither, Lady Mackay.' Amethyst's answer was quietly given and then she smiled, deep dimples evident in each cheek and a knowing humour across her face.

Strength and honour had its own allure, Daniel thought, watching her deflect the other's interest with such acumen. Out here in the open with the promise of a ride before them and a beautiful summer's evening foretelling a hopeful outlook, Charlotte looked overdressed and overdone. However, as if realising that she would have little more in the way of conversation from Amethyst, she turned her attention towards him.

'I will be here tomorrow at the same time. Perhaps we might enjoy a ride alone.' Her hand closed over Daniel's sleeve and in her inimitable style she leaned across to him, the riding habit she wore cut as low as it could be. 'For old times' sake. For the world that was before it all turned different. For us,' she whispered closely, the breath of her words across his face daring more.

Once he might have smiled back his assent and followed her to the ends of the earth. But that was then and this was now. Amethyst Cameron had looked away, her eyes on the trees far in the distance as the horse below her shuffled.

Tipping his hat to both ladies he disengaged

Charlotte's grasp and made his steed walk on. When they were out of earshot he tried to explain.

'Lady Mackay is lonely and—'

Amethyst interrupted him. 'I don't require an explanation, my lord. I won't be that sort of wife.'

He laughed, but the sound was not humorous. 'Then what sort of wife will you be, Miss Cameron?

She did not answer, but the red flush of anger on her face was telling and what had been a comfortable and easy meeting was suddenly difficult. But he needed to explain to her honestly so that she did not imagine he would be a philandering husband.

'We were lovers for three-and-a-half years between the stints of my army duty.' Now she looked around at him. 'I was twenty-seven when I met Charlotte and thirty when she ran off and married Lord Spenser Mackay. He was an extremely wealthy Scottish landowner, you understand, and I was a second son and a soldier.'

'So she broke your heart?'

His laughter this time was much more genuine. 'At the time perhaps I thought that she had.'

'But now...?'

'Now with the wisdom of distance there is the greatest relief in the realisation that we would never have suited.'

'I got the impression that she thinks exactly the opposite.'

'Then she is wrong.' The distance had returned to his voice. 'Do you have a ball dress?'

'Yes. Why?'

'There is a ball on Saturday night which will be well attended. I hope you might accompany me to it?'

'Would your family be there?'

'No. Mama has a slight cold and my two sisters are still young.' He hesitated for a moment. 'I thought you might have known all my particular familial circumstances when you made me your choice of groom?'

For the first time he heard Amethyst laugh as though she meant it. She simply tossed her head back and sounded happy. He was mesmerised.

'I left the snooping to my father, my lord.'

'And I passed muster?'

'It was the time you spent with Sir John Moore in La Corunna that sealed it for my father, I think. It was said that you were quite the hero on the heights of Penasquedo and he has always admired those who might lay down their life for crown and country, you see.'

'And what of your choice?'

The good humour vanished in a second.

'I no longer trust myself enough to make wise decisions.'

'Which implies that you have made some foolish ones?'

'People change on you when you least expect it, my lord.' She looked at him directly now, the dark of her eyes marked with a softer gold.

'Aye, that they do. Lady Mackay became a woman I did not recognise, but I wouldn't say her intransigence was my problem.'

The small show of her dimples heartened him. 'The blame was hers, you mean.'

'Entirely.'

'And you moved on without looking back?' she asked curiously.

'I did.'

This conversation was taking a surprising turn. Honesty was something she favoured and Lord Daniel Wylde had not held back about his past or lied about it.

Unlike her.

Such knowledge shrivelled her good mood,

though their kiss of the other day still lingered below each glance and word. A scorching and undeniable truth embracing neither logic nor reason.

Passing into a narrower path, he took the reins of her horse and pulled them both to a stop. 'Even given the unusual circumstances of our union, Miss Cameron, I want us to be friends.'

Friends. As she had been at first with Gerald Whitely. She hoped he did not see the consternation on her face because what he was offering was honourable.

'I certainly would not wish for two years of bickering.'

She shook her head. Everything he said made perfect sense and she had come into this betrothal only with the expectation of filling the last months of her father's life with happiness. But the kiss they had shared had skewed things, made them different and she could not help but hope that he might eschew convention and take her in his arms, here in the most public of places. That he might kiss her again, show her it had not been all a figment of her imagination, fill in the empty fears with a warm certainty.

But of course he did not, he merely called his horse on and challenged her.

'You ride well, Miss Cameron. At Montcliffe after we are married I would deem it an honour to pit my horse against your own.'

She gave him a smile, her roan shimmying as she let her attention wander. With Montcliffe beside her and the summer breeze in her face Amythest felt the sort of freedom that she had missed for months now.

'I think for a fair competition you would have to allow me a starting distance. Your mount looks as if he might beat anything he was up against.'

He laughed and the sound was honest and true. 'Deimos here was well blooded in the Peninsular Campaign in Spain.'

'Deimos?' she repeated the name. 'The Grecian spirit of dread and terror?'

He smiled. 'Not many would know that.'

'You took him to the Continent?'

'I rode with the Eighteenth Light Dragoons under Lord Paget.'

'Is that where you hurt your leg?'

'On the last day at La Corunna. The medic couldn't get the bullet out.'

'So it is still in there?' she asked, horrified.

'And hurting like hell.' Unexpectedly he smiled. 'I don't usually talk about the injury and certainly seldom admit to any pain.'

'Why do you not simply have the shot removed then? Here, in London?'

'The surgeon said that it lay near an artery. If they accidentally severed it during the operation, I should lose either my leg or my life, so at this stage the option of doing nothing is the sensible one. Besides, to complete my side of the marriage deal I still need to scare people away from your father, Miss Cameron.'

'I think you could do that anyway, Lord Montcliffe, with one leg or two.'

'Do you?' His demeanour had changed. Now he leant towards her, taking the bridle to hold her mare still. She felt the blood in her cheeks rise as it never had before, so red that her whole face throbbed with the consternation.

'I like it when you blush.'

Daniel Wylde was lethal. With just a few words he could make her forget everything and believe in fairy tales with happy endings against impossible odds.

Better to remember the way Charlotte Mackay had looked at her with that innate snobbery so prevalent in the English upper classes as she had sniffed out the presence of trade like a bloodhound. Tomorrow when the notice of their intention to marry went into the papers Amethyst could hardly bear to think of what the repercussions would be. But the very worst of it was that she wanted this man before her, wanted his kisses, his smiles and his compliments, no matter what.

'The ball you speak of, would it be very formal?' she asked apprehensively.

'It would indeed. Did they ever teach you how to dance at your Gaskell Street Presbyterian Church School.'

'They taught me what they knew, though there were times when I wondered just how much that actually was.'

'Did you learn how to waltz?'

'No.'

'A pity, for they call it the dance of love.' Now his amusement was easily seen. 'If you like, I would be most happy to teach you the steps.'

He loved the way she was so easily flustered, this woman of commerce and business and brusqueness, though his attention was caught by a series of heavy pins around the line of her hair that had been dislodged by the movement of the ride.

'Do you wear a wig?'

Her fingers instantly came up to where it was he looked, pushing the dull brown hair forward in one easy swipe.

'I do.' Her hand shook as she tried to secure the loosened clips.

'Why?' Surprise at her admission had him frowning.

'The accident in the carriage that we told you of. I had my head shaved so that the surgeon could drill into my scalp to release the pressure on my brain.'

My God. No simple accident, then, but an operation that could have so easily killed her. He tried to hide his concern and concentrated on the fact that she had survived. 'What colour is the hair beneath?'

'Not this shade.' The lowering sun radiated on her face, altering the plain sallowness of her complexion. 'It is lighter. And curlier. I did not think it would take this long to grow back, though, so I retrieved this old hairpiece from my mother's things. Now I regret it. But on saying so I do not wish you to think I am vain, it's just that….' She stopped, her teeth worrying her bottom lip and confusion sending her eyes away from his.

Sometimes she looked so unexpectedly beautiful that for the first time since he had met her he allowed himself to imagine something finer between them, his sex swelling with the promise. Amethyst Amelia Cameron was honest to a fault and forthright and direct. She did not simper or lie or pretend. He was so very sick of the deceit of women, that was the trouble. Charlotte Mackay had for ever cured him of liars and his sisters and mother had done the rest with their duplicity and falsities.

He wished they were somewhere else, somewhere quiet and private, some place that he might bring her up against him and reassure her that he did not think she was vain, but the pathways of the park were filling with more riders and the crease on her forehead told him that she was as astonished as he by their candour.

'We should go back.'

She glanced away from him and nodded, her fingers tense on the leather reins and every nail bitten to the quick. He wondered why she did not wear the riding gloves he could so plainly see tucked into the fold of her belt.

* * *

The dream came again that night of the carriage turning over, the scream of the horses and the cold of the day. Her hand had been caught by her thick woollen glove against a seat that had come loose and she could not free herself and jump to safety as her father had done.

Over and over and over, in the slow motion of fear. She had not lost consciousness when her head slammed against the roof or lapsed into a faint as her wrist had broken. No, she had lain there as the dust settled, the bright stream of blood turning the day to red and listening to the last dying breaths of one of the horses.

Her father had reached her first and by his expression she knew things must have been bad. 'My broken doll,' he had whispered, words so unlike his usual diction she had thought she must already be dead.

But the pain came later, as did the fear of heavy gloves, and carriage speed and long-distance travelling. Unreasonable, she knew, but nevertheless there. She had seen Daniel look at her bare hands and wonder.

Her fingers went up to feel her hair. It was finally growing, a good amount of curl now covering the pink baldness of her scalp. She could have almost dispensed with the wig altogether, but it had become a sort of disguise that she liked in the time since she had put it on and now she was loathe to simply do away with it. People did not notice her as they once had. She blended in more, the colour of the hairpiece picking up some tone in her skin that kept her hidden. She could walk amongst a crowd and barely feel a glance.

Her tresses had once been her crowning glory. Gerald Whitely told her that time and time again before she had married him. Afterwards he had barely mentioned it, the long silences between them hurtful and unending.

A light tap on her door had her pulling the neck of her nightgown up.

'Come in.'

Her father walked forward, the silver cane the only vestige of his fall the other evening, though he leant on it with quite some force.

'I saw the light under your door.'

'You could not sleep either?'

He shook his head. 'You seem out of sorts lately and I keep wondering whether this marriage agreement is the cause of it? Lord Montcliffe is after all quite forceful and if you should wish to nullify—'

'No, Papa.' She cut across his words and watched his face light up. 'I am quite happy with things as they are.'

'It is just the marriage notice will be in the paper tomorrow and I should imagine after that things might change a little.'

'Lord Montcliffe said the same this afternoon when we were riding. He asked me to a ball on Saturday evening, a formal occasion with much of society in attendance.'

'And you agreed?'

'He made it difficult to refuse.'

Her father sat down on the chair opposite and wiped his brow. 'I am uncertain of the ways of all this. Perhaps we should employ a chaperone for you, Amethyst, so that we don't get things wrong.'

'I do not think it will be necessary, Papa. We will repair to Dunstan House as soon as we are married and then we need not worry at all.'

'Montcliffe is amenable to that?'

'He once told us that he would be. Besides, a friend of his, the Earl of Ross, asked if his sister might be able to assist in the preparation for the wedding. Perhaps I could also ask her for a little assistance with the ball as well. It seems she is most creative with these things and I have a few gowns that could be altered to make them more fashionable without too much trouble.'

The smile on her father's face was bright with relief. He looked happier than he had been in a long while.

'If we had some notion of how many people would attend your marriage ceremony, that would also be of a help. The contract stated the marriage would take place before the end of July and the weeks will run away if we do not get it all in hand.'

'It will be a small group, Papa. No more than twenty.'

'But the Montcliffe family will be there?'

'I am not sure, Papa. They all seem distant from one another.

'A shame that, for family is all you have to rely on in the world when it comes down to it.'

'I am uncertain Lord Montcliffe would agree as he seldom speaks of his.'

'Well, I shall send them invites, nonetheless, for it is only good manners.'

A sense of dread began to play in Amethyst's mind. Would the Montcliffes be difficult? Would they accept her? Would they come? Only a few weeks until her wedding and she still had not procured a dress. Tomorrow she would send a note to Lady Christine Howard to see if she might consent to help her.

'You are marrying whom?' His mother's voice was shrill and disbelieving.

Both his sisters sat very still at the dinner table, their eating utensils poised to listen.

'Miss Amethyst Amelia Cameron.'

'And you say her father is a man of trade?'

'Mr Robert Cameron is a successful timber merchant and is far wealthier than the Montcliffes have any hope of ever being.'

He hated that he should have to qualify his choice of bride in monetary value, but it seemed such an explanation was all Janet Montcliffe understood. She looked furious.

'Amethyst? What sort of name is that?'

'Hers.' Daniel was tired of being careful and polite. His mother's frown deepened.

'We will be the laughing stock of the *ton*.'

'I doubt that sincerely, Mother.'

'Do you love her, then?' This question came from his oldest sister Gwen, the sort of light shining in her eyes that could only belong to a naive and unworldly girl.

'Of course he does not.' His mother answered for him. 'The interloper has simply tipped her cap at the title and managed to do what a hundred well-brought-up daughters of society have not been able to. She has brought your brother to heel and he will regret it, mark my words. You are marrying well beneath your station in life, Daniel, but any remorse afterwards will be useless. You will be tied to the upstart for life.'

'I am taking it that you will not be attending the wedding ceremony then, Mother?'

'None of us will be. I could not bear to look on Miss Amethyst Cameron's face and see the gleam of victory within it. The girls should not be allowed anywhere near such…*tradespeople* either.' She almost spat the word out. 'As for your grandfather, he is sick and hasn't the energy for all this nonsense so you are alone in your foolish choice of bride. I had such high hopes for you, too.'

Daniel stood as the resulting silence lengthened. 'Then I shall bid you goodnight.'

With that he simply walked to the door and left.

He found himself lingering in the confines of Grosvenor Square. The Cameron house was dark save for a light on the second floor where the curtains had been drawn. The shadow of a woman caught in candlelight moved in a way that made him frown. His wife-to-be was dancing alone in her room and the outline showed no sign of the shape of her wig. A waltz, he determined by the beat of steps she took, a practice of the dance of love.

The tension he felt began to lessen and lighting a cheroot he leant back and watched. Janet Montcliffe and her bitterness had been a constant in his life, the anger and the rancour almost normal.

Amethyst Cameron, unlike his mother, was a logical and reasonable woman and one who held to the tenet of wording differences of opinion in a sane and sensible way. She did not whine or moan or berate. He liked her smile and her dimples and the low timbre of her voice. Her clothes might be shapeless and ill-formed but when the wind had caught her riding attire and pressed the material against her body he saw that there was a surprisingly shapely form beneath. He was intrigued by the description of her hair. Light and curly. Velvet-brown eyes would complement such a shade admirably.

After the scene at the dinner table tonight he wished he was anywhere but in London town. A different life was one he had been dreaming of for quite a while now. He smiled as the shadow drifted closer to the window and hoped she might pull the curtain back to look down and see him.

He liked talking to her. He liked her blushes and the quiet way she had dealt with the snobbery of Lady Charlotte Mackay. He liked her father.

Breathing out heavily, he wondered what all this meant.

He had always felt homeless, but Amethyst Cameron had had the effect of anchoring him. His father had been a man who was melancholic and weak and as his bitterness grew he had sworn that no offspring from his unhappy marriage would ever see a penny of the family money. An unhappy coupling that had brought out the worst in both of them, Daniel suddenly reasoned, and the thought made him drop his cigar beneath his boot and stomp out the embers. Nigel and he had been caught in the crossfire of their parents' shortcomings. The spending of great sums of money and long holidays apart had dammed up the resentments for a while, but even that had not altered their basic dislike of each other. When his father had fallen from his horse after a long drinking binge his mother had buried him with a smile on her face.

Daniel did not look back as he strode into Upper Brook Street and hailed a passing cabriolet.

Chapter Six

'No, this is a far better colour on you, Amethyst. See how the gold brings out the shade in your eyes.' Lady Christine Howard smiled as she wound a darker gold band about the neckline. 'With just a bit of manoeuvring we can lower the bodice and attach it. If I fashion it carefully, it will fold like this to show off your curves.'

Lord Ross's sister was like a small whirlwind, her clever fingers pushing the fabric into a shape that was indeed flattering.

'You do not think it a little daring?'

'Absolutely not. Compared to some of the other gowns on display you will look like a novice newly released from a French convent.' Christine laughed loudly and Amethyst joined in. Nowhere at all lingered the depression or sadness that her brother had spoken of, though the large ruby ring she wore on her marriage finger alluded to a lost betrothed.

'The trick of it is to believe you are the most beautiful woman in the room and act like it.'

Amethyst's face fell. Such a thing sounded impossibly difficult.

'Your hair will need to be done differently, of course, to have any hope of pulling it off. The wig must go.'

'You knew I wore one?'

'Does not everybody? You could look so much prettier than you do now with it gone and I love the art of dressing hair.'

Like a shop dress form, Amethyst was pulled this way and that and the strangest thing of it all was that she was beginning to actually enjoy the unfamiliar pampering and the rapid conversation.

'Your husband-to-be has most of the women of the *ton* panting after him and why would he not, for he is beautiful.'

'Too beautiful for me.'

The words were out before she realised she had said them, but Christine appeared completely unfazed.

'You hide what you have, that is the trouble,

but it is time to come out from the shadows. More importantly you have a fortune and is that not what all of the men of the *ton* need these days? I know Lucien does. It is a great pity you do not have a sister for then he could marry her and we would be related and no longer poor. I do hate how money, or rather the lack of it, defines one.'

'In my circle of acquaintances it doesn't, really.'

'That is why you are such a refreshing find, Amethyst, and why I like being here to help you.'

Christine reached into the case she had brought with her for another piece of fabric, this time the lightest shade of red and held it to Amy's face. 'Next time you buy a gown, choose this shade. See how it suits your skin? What colour is your real hair, by the way, or do you have none?'

Because there was no artifice or malice in the question Amy undid the pins and lifted the dull brown wig away, fluffing out her curls beneath.

'There was a carriage accident,' she explained as Christine stood in silence. 'It has only just begun to grow back properly again.'

'I did not expect you to be so blonde,' the other woman finally said. 'Has Montcliffe seen you without your wig?'

'No.'

The resulting laughter worried her. 'Then we will be able to greatly surprise him come Saturday and I for one cannot wait to see the look on Lady Charlotte Mackay's face when she understands what she is up against.'

'I have met her already.'

'Where?'

'In the park riding the other day. She barely talked to me.'

'That is because she is formidable and scary and so are all her friends. So be warned, while she is undeniably beautiful, she also finds people's weaknesses and uses them to her full advantage. Word has it she wants Lord Montcliffe back and will do anything to achieve her goal, so don't be fooled. Beneath her pale and refined appearance lies a character of pure steel.'

'She would not have been pleased to see our marriage notice in the paper, then?'

'Indeed. It is a wonder Lady Mackay has not been around here already saying all that she imagines you would want to hear whilst searching around for the secrets that you don't want revealed.'

Gerald Whitely.

The thought struck Amethyst with a blinding ferocity. How easy would it be for her to find out about him? A cloud of worry descended, though when Christine brought forth a folded cloth threaded with glass-headed pins, she decided not to think about her many problems.

Gerald belonged in the past and that is where she wished for him to stay. Nobody in the *ton* had the slightest idea of who the Camerons were and where they had come from. She would tell Daniel, of course, about her first husband and a few of her reasons for being most grateful when he had died, but that was all.

Perhaps she could have a conversation with him about it all at the ball on Saturday. If she asked the Earl to take her home afterwards that might give her a moment of privacy to try to make him understand the nature of her past.

When Christine indicated that she had finished attaching the band of cloth to her gown Amy turned to the mirror and was astonished. The gold in the silken cloth brought out the colour in her eyes and her hair and made her complexion appear almost flawless.

'I cannot believe that this is me.'

'It will be even better on Saturday,' her new friend returned, 'because I will put your hair up like this and fashion it with flowers.'

Clever fingers arranged the curls in a way that gave the impression of far more hair than she had and Amethyst smiled.

'See,' Christine exclaimed. 'With a simple smile everything comes together in exactly the way that it should.'

On the evening of the Herringworth ball Daniel Wylde and Lucien Howard waited in the salon downstairs with Robert Cameron.

'My daughter will be down presently. Your sister, Lord Ross, is helping her to dress as we speak and I have been banned from going anywhere near the upstairs bed chambers.'

Looking at a clock on the opposite wall, Daniel nodded. It was still considered early in society terms and so they had all the time in the world to wait. Besides the brandy that Robert had plied them with upon their arrival was both smooth and rich.

He wondered as he took the first sip whether he should have asked his sister Gwen to help Christine with Amethyst's preparation for the ball, but dismissed the thought as most unworkable. Perhaps after the wedding he could make certain that both Gwen and Caroline spent more time with them at either Montcliffe Manor or Dunstan House in the hope that his mother's influence over the young girls might lessen. He envied Lucien for the smooth ease of the Howard family dynamics, in spite of Lucien's contrary grandfather.

'I have not known Amethyst to take quite this much trouble with her appearance before.' Robert Cameron was peering at the clock.

'It will be the influence of my sister, Mr Cameron, for she is meticulous in her observation of detail. Your daughter will not have a chance to take breath once Christine hits her stride.'

'Well, people and things have been coming and going all day, my lords. Let us pray she won't be disappointed with the outcome for her hair is still so...' He stopped and fidgeted with the brandy bottle, seeming uncertain in the present company as to whether he should go on or not.

'Short.' Daniel finished the sentence off. 'She told me of it whilst we were riding in the park the other day.'

Robert Cameron smiled and leant back in his chair. He was still far too thin, but he looked healthier and more relaxed. 'Then that is a relief to hear, for I doubt my daughter has confided in anybody else and sometimes I wish she would.'

'You have no other relatives at all?'

'None. I was an only child and so was Susannah.'

Daniel thought for a moment how freeing that must be in the light of all the difficulties with his mother. Lucien's frown had deepened, though. The Howards had generally always been a close-knit family and he was probably wondering at how the Camerons could have been so isolated. Robert, however, was expounding on their aloneness in a voice that sounded worried.

'The business has taken much of our time, you see, but in the past week I have sold a great deal of it off to a competitor who has always expressed an interest in buying it. I hope now that Dunstan House might be my principal place of residence, a quieter life with the horses, you understand. A home where we might become part of a community.'

Their conversation was interrupted by a butler who appeared at the door. 'Miss Cameron and Lady Christine have instructed me to tell you that they are ready, sir.'

The rustle of silk was followed by small steps on the marble floor and then his wife-to-be was before him. Daniel could barely recognise her.

Gone was the dull brown lustreless wig, replaced by light blonde curls tucked up into a band of small yellow roses, the honey, straw and gold of her tresses making her dark eyes and eyebrows stand out in a way they had not before. In the light of the candles her skin looked transparent, the previously sallow tone of her skin transformed now into almost alabaster.

Daniel found himself on his feet, speechless at the transformation. Her golden gown clung too, displaying the curves only hinted at in the shapeless clothes she normally favoured. She filled out the bodice of her dress admirably though her waist was tiny. When she saw where he looked she began to speak immediately.

'Christine assures me that this neckline is most tasteful and not at all racy and that other women wear far more revealing outfits.' Her fingers tugged at the darker shade of material that swathed the bodice. Gloves, the lightest of gossamer lace, barely covered the glow of her skin.

'You look...different.' He hardly recognised his own voice as the dimples marking her cheeks deepened, her bones elegant and sculpted in the light. Her lips were painted with a quiet pink and it emphasised the fullness of them. He could barely breathe properly with the transformation.

Palms open, she gestured to the dress. 'This is the result of hours and hours of work on Christine's behalf, I am afraid, my lord. Tomorrow I shall be just as I was.'

But for Daniel time seemed to stand still, caught in astonishment and trepidation. Before Amethyst Cameron might have been largely invisible in a society ballroom, but now...now the knives could be out and sharper than they might otherwise have been.

When he glanced across he could see the same sort of astonishment on Lucien's face that must have been evident upon his own. Christine simply looked as though she might laugh out loud.

God, he wished they did not have to go out at all, society and its expectations bearing down upon them with all its infatuation with beauty and grace. Her father was watching him too, eyes keen and his smile broad, giving Daniel the impression that he had known all along how truly lovely his daughter was.

'I think we should ask Lady Christine to help again in the preparation for the wedding day, my dear. You have not looked so pretty in an age and I want a full report tomorrow on all the happenings at the ball,' Robert said.

Only pretty? Daniel swallowed the words back and looked over at Lucien. There was a definite challenge in his green eyes.

'I am more than certain tonight shall prove a most interesting experience, Mr Cameron.' Lucien's drawl was slow and languid.

'Lord Montcliffe, Miss Amethyst Cameron, Lord Ross and Lady Christine Howard.'

As their names rang out across the ballroom the conversations filling the generous space quietened and heads turned their way.

This was exactly what Amethyst had been dreading, this exposure coupled with a public knowledge that she was from the lowly echelons of trade. She held in her breath and wondered if she might ever release it.

'I always pretend there is a field of grass before me at this moment,' Christine trilled, 'and that the colourful gowns are flowers. And I never look anyone in the eye.'

Despite her trepidation Amethyst smiled and the awful horror of being so very visible faded into something she was more able to cope with. Daniel did not look even vaguely nonplussed by all the attention. Rather he seemed almost bored, an Earl who had graced countless ballrooms and endless society functions just like this.

His world, Amethyst thought. His heritage. Today he wore a large ring on the first finger of his left hand. She had not noticed him sport any jewellery before and this one was substantial— the crest impaled with a lion in red on one half and a series of white crosses in gold on the other. The family badges of a noble birth passed down from father to son. Just another small token of an exalted lineage and a further example of how unsuitably matched they were.

She had decided in the end not to wear any jewellery at all, letting the golden gown speak for itself with its intricate folds and detailing, but in this room with all the glamour of the *ton* she wondered if such lack was a mistake. Here, she felt out of place, the lessons from Gaskell Street leaving her totally unprepared for such opulence. She wanted to take Daniel's hand and hold it close, an anchor in a world that was foreign and a man who could easily overcome any difficulties. But she did not, of course, for he had moved away slightly, making no attempt to claim her.

As they came to the group of people standing at the bottom of the steps she smiled politely and waited for Daniel to speak.

'When did you get back, Francis?' he asked one of the men.

'This afternoon.'

'And your cousin?'

'Was long gone and had left no word of her return.' His eyes flicked towards Amethyst, the startling depths of hazel guarded and questioning. 'The *ton* is abuzz with your news, Montcliffe. Rather hasty, I might add, given that when I saw you last week you made no mention of a would-be wife.'

Lucien laughed. 'The call of rich and beautiful is a strong one, Francis, as I am sure you must appreciate. Were you not on exactly the same mission in Bath?'

The words were both familiar and strange to Amethyst. Lord Ross could hardly think her beautiful, but she was rich. And was this Francis trying to find his own wealthy intended?

Of a sudden the hazel eyes of the stranger softened and he bowed his head towards her.

A mark of war lashed the newcomer's left cheek in one cruel and unbroken line, leaving her to wonder at the pain that such a wound must have inflicted. If he noticed her looking, he made no reaction to show that he cared.

'We were all at school together and followed each other to the battlefields,' Daniel explained. 'Overfamiliarity sometimes breeds a contempt of manners, but I am certain my friend will remember his soon.'

This time a true smile creased the ruined face. 'I beg your pardon for my rudeness, Miss Cameron. My name is Lord Francis St Cartmail, Earl of Douglas, and I am more than interested to know if you have sisters?'

'I have already explored that avenue, Francis,' Christine quickly informed him. 'For my brother, you understand. But sadly she is an only child.'

'Then we still have to find our own fortunes, Luce.'

Laughter ensued, mirth that was neither embarrassed nor apologetic. The sort of laughter that told Amethyst these were friends who were in it for the long haul, thick or thin, good or bad. And it seemed that each warrior before her was also facing financial ruin.

The war, she wondered, or the war wounds? It cannot have been easy for them to come back into the glittering perfection of the *ton* from the hell of a Peninsular Campaign. Who would understand what they had been through and what they had seen, save for those who had returned with them. Forging bonds, closing the ranks. There was an ease in shared sorrow.

Compared to these three, the other men here looked effeminate and affected. She also saw the interest of many of the ladies in the assembly stray in their direction, some glances hopeful and shy whilst others were more bold and direct. When Daniel's arm unexpectedly touched hers she looked down, his large fingers encased in a glove, the fabric of his jacket contrasting against her shimmering gown. A connection, amidst all the movement and chatter, the spark of a vibrating energy running into her fingers. Almost burning.

He must have felt it too because he pulled away, the contact lost, but not before she saw shock in his eyes.

A waltz began to be played by a string quartet stationed at the head of the room. A Viennese waltz played quickly. She had danced to this in her room in Mayfair as a practice. Back-two-three. Back-two-three. Her heart raced even faster when Daniel turned and asked her to dance.

Daniel found it difficult to know exactly what to make of Miss Amethyst Cameron as she came into his arms, her wheat-gold curls piled beneath yellow rosebuds and the gown of a darker hue sending the shade of her eyes to a burnished velvet.

She did not look as if she belonged here amidst the *ton* and the ballroom and the vacuous pursuits of those with little else save social soirées to occupy their time. She was so much more than that—an interloper who would bide here for a while just to watch it all.

It was the strength in her that made the others look weaker, he decided, for women who needed men to survive had a certain brittle incompetence that was shown up by Amethyst's independence. His arms tightened about her.

'Thank you for coming.'

'You thought I might not?'

He smiled and led her into the dance. 'I watched you practising the waltz the other night from the street. Your shadow had fallen against the curtain.'

Her breath stilled, puzzlement making her pull back a little. 'Why were you there?'

'I was walking. I walk sometimes when I cannot sleep and when the sense of life is questionable. My wanderings brought me to Grosvenor Square.'

'Then, given our unusual marriage contract, you must have found yourself exercising a lot of late, my lord. I might add that practice does not make one perfect so I hope my lack of prowess as a dancer doesn't disappoint you.'

The imbalance was back, clawing into reason, her eyes full of laughter tonight and as close as they had been when he'd kissed her. He wanted to again. God, how he wanted to.

'This marriage is not all about the money, Miss Cameron. Your father's offer was unexpected and generous, but…' He stopped and looked away.

'You did not have to take it?'

Shaking his head, he brought her closer, but wrapped together in the arms of a crowded room there was so little space to be honest.

He liked the way she smelt and felt, he liked how her head fitted just beneath his chin and how the warmth of her skin came through the gossamer lace of her gloves.

Perfect.

Hell, he was turning into a man he did not recognise, the soldier in him submerged beneath another force. He could feel her breath against his throat, too, and the small intimacy held him in thrall.

'Your hair looks nice.' He could have phrased it better, he supposed, could have talked of the colour or the curl or the way it matched her skin, could have used the flowery words that women were supposed to like. But she answered before he could dredge up more.

'Christine hid the shortness in the flowers.' Her eyes met his own. 'It must be exhausting to be a constant part of an assembly such as this, my lord? So much attention upon us and so much expectation.'

'It hasn't always been so. In the army I was largely free of it. My older brother was the one in the public eye and I left him to it.'

'When did he die?'

'Almost eighteen months ago now in an accident whilst out hunting at Montcliffe.'

'Perhaps he was not as happy as you thought him to be, for the dubious habits of gambling and fast living don't point to a man at peace with himself.'

Daniel hoped his laughter did not sound too unkind. 'The duty of an Earldom rules out many of those personal luxuries. He was supposed to be protecting the Montcliffe name, not gambling it away to anyone who would meet him at the card table. When he lost, Montcliff Manor lost as well.'

'It was sold?'

'No, I have largely closed the place up for now. Most of the servants were given their notice, but I have kept on a very small staff.' He had hated taking livelihoods away from people who had worked at Montcliffe Manor for years and whose great-great-grandfathers and grandmothers had toiled at the same job in other centuries.

'Your brother wasn't a champion of family heritage, then. My father has tried to inject tradition at Dunstan House even though the history is not our own.'

'What's it like?'

'Beautiful. It is made of honey-coloured stone and sits behind a lake. My father wrote a poem about it when we first went there and I had it framed.'

'Only one?'

She laughed. 'He never took to the pen again in such a descriptive way. *"The rooks swarming and the swallows skimming and the oak trees reflecting in the lake."* My mother would have loved it.'

'But she had died by then?'

'Yes. When I was eight.'

'So it was always just the two of you?'

'It was. Just us, and that is why Papa…' She stopped, a line of worry etched into her brow.

'Why he is so important to you? Why you wish for him to be happy?'

The music swirled about them, the notes of the violinists to one end of the room plaintive. Amethyst had never heard such music played before, but everything about tonight had been like a dream and Daniel's hand across her gossamer-silk gloves made her feel different.

Even with his injured leg he danced well, the quiet push of his body against hers as he led her around the floor. If his brother Nigel had been weak and fickle, Daniel was strong and solid and good, a man who would protect his family with all that he had, a soldier who had fought for crown and country and had spilled his blood in doing so. A husband as unlike Gerald in every way that it was possible to be.

The thought made the breath in her throat shallow. Here in the midst of society in the bosom of a group who could so easily revile her, she felt safe and protected in Daniel's arms. But she needed to tell him of her first marriage before much longer, needed to make him understand that such a mistake sometimes left you floundering for the right words and the proper explanations. A further reflection made her stiffen. Gerald's business deals had taken him into the world of the *ton*. Perhaps some here had even met him. The room felt suddenly warm.

'Your friend Lucien mentioned that you once bred horses?' she asked, trying to push her anxiety aside for now.

'I did indeed, at Montcliffe, before I sold most of them and bought a commission into the army. Deimos was the only one left of that line.'

'You will like the stable at Dunstan House, then. Papa has not held back in buying the best of livestock, although lately he has lost interest in the project because of his health. The Arabian greys were a part of his big plan.'

'Yet he looked more robust tonight.'

The sentiment made her smile. 'I think it is your influence, my lord, and I thank you for it.'

His fingers tightened on her own. 'I need to find you a ring. Is there any stone you might favour?'

She shook her head. 'I seldom wear jewellery.'

'There was a large diamond ring at the bottom of the bag you left at my town house. When I lifted it the contents fell out.'

Gerald's ring. The one he had given her when he had pledged eternal love and loyalty in the chapel at Gaskell Street. He had won it at cards, she was to find out later, from a man who had stolen it from his sister in order to stay at the tables. A symbol as broken as its promise. She had forgotten she had even thrown it into her cloth bag where it had lain forgotten until the night Daniel had kissed her.

'I dislike diamonds.' She tried to keep the anger from her voice.

'Then you must be the only woman in the entire room who does.'

'And I prefer my hands bare of any adornment.'

So nothing can catch. So that the gloves she

wore in public could easily slip off at the end of an event.

'Because of the scars on your wrist?'

He had noticed? She thought that even through the sheer silk and lace they had been hidden. The skin above muscle torn away from bone was healed now, but there were other scars that would never mend.

Missing a step, she fell against Montcliffe, his strength gathering her in and holding her steady.

'Everyone harbours secrets, Amethyst.'

She liked the way he said her Christian name, with that precise accent of privilege. She also liked the way his breath fell against her scalp, the soft whisper of her freed curls so different from the heavy cloying feeling of the wig.

She noticed others watching them, some covertly and others more directly. If she could, she would have closed her eyes and only felt Daniel's arms about her, the steady beat of his heart, the smell of strength and maleness and honour. She wished her father might have been here to watch the pageantry and the beauty, the chandeliers above, the violinists in the leafy grotto, the women dancing, bedecked in every colour of the rainbow, jewels sparkling in the flame.

A different life and so very far removed from ledgers and order books and the brisk trading of timber. So very different from Gerald, too, with his heavy fists and his angry ranting, all the faults in the world everyone else's save his own.

Her father would have loved to have seen her enjoying a night like this, being a part of society in a way he had never imagined she would.

Here in this room it was beauty that was most remarkable, the old lines of tradition and the mark of history holding its own kind of thrall. Swallowing back a growing delight she let Lord Montcliffe guide her around the floor.

As he caught his sore leg on an intricate step Daniel was pleased when the music ceased. He needed a drink badly, the back of his throat dry and a dread in his stomach that he remembered from the battlefields.

No control. No damn certainty. Amethyst was his bride of convenience and yet here he was, falling under her spell. Like a green boy. Unmistakably stupid. Two years she had made him promise until they could end it all. Just a union of utility to benefit her father and his family. How much plainer could she state it?

Francis handed him a drink when they were once again back within the group. A fine smooth brandy that did away with the foolishness. He made certain that he did not stand next to his wife-to-be, slipping into the space between his two best friends instead. His leg ached and throbbed, but there were other parts of his body too that were bursting into a life long since deadened.

He wanted Miss Amethyst Amelia Cameron. He did. He wanted to lie down with her in their marriage bed for all the hours of all the nights of his life and listen to her heartbeat. She was honest and real and true. A woman who did not lie or simper or deceive.

God, what would it be like to live with a woman who did not use every waking hour to plan the next gown or soirée as his sisters and mother were prone to, their constant gossip and ever-present fits of displeasure marring this day and then the next one.

Simple. Uncomplicated. Truthful.

When Gabriel Hughes came towards them with his sister and mother in tow, Daniel frowned. Charlotte looked as beautiful as ever, but she no longer held any sway over him. Tonight he could not even see what her attraction must have been.

'We meet again, Lord Montcliffe. It is becoming a habit, though of course your marriage notice in the paper was a decided surprise. To a lot of people, I expect, your mother included. I can't imagine she was pleased.' Her voice was hard, an edge of anger upon it and another thing that he could not name.

Amethyst was listening, as was Christine, though Lucien was trying to make a decent fist of a conversation with them to give him some privacy.

With her blue eyes flashing Charlotte Mackay used her words like swords, the sharp point of meaning aimed true. She knew Janet Montcliffe had always favoured an alliance between them, two pre-eminent families of the *ton* melded into an ordained partnership. Any association with the world of trade was as offensive to Charlotte as it was to his mother and she made no attempt whatsoever to conceal her feelings.

Gabe and Lady Wesley looked less sure as to the purpose of such an outburst. Indeed, her mother was trying to pull Charlotte away, her teeth set in a rigid smile of fluster, but her daughter was having none of it.

'I should like to ask Miss Cameron a question if I may, my lord.' The silky tone of her words signalled danger and the group around them fell into silence. 'I would like to ask her if she knew a man called Mr Whitely?

The bottom fell out of Amethyst's world, a single terrible thump of something breaking into a thousand shards of shame and all the more dreadful because it was so unexpected and public.

'Mr Gerald Whitely?' She hated the way her voice sounded as she echoed the words back, but she needed to give herself a moment to think.

'Your husband, Miss Cameron, or should I say Mrs Whitely. The man you married. Surely you remember him?'

'Oh, you have it very wrong, Lady Hughes, for she is not spoken for. Miss Cameron is about to be married in the next few weeks to Lord Montcliffe and I think…' Christine's sentiments broke across the growing silence, petering out as she realised with amazement that the accusations could actually be true.

'Gerald Whitely? The name is familiar.' Lord Ross's voice came through the fog. 'Was he not the one who set up a company early last year to swindle wealthy investors out of their funds?'

'Amethyst?' Daniel spoke now, the timbre in his voice drawn, and when she looked up his pale eyes were icy.

'It…is a…mistake.' She could barely get the words out.

'Then perhaps the *ton* would like to hear why a married woman should insist on using her maiden name when her true one might elicit howls of derision.' Charlotte's tone rang with victory though it hollowed as her brother bundled her up and pulled her away, his mouth grimly set.

'You have said your piece, Charlotte. It is now time to leave.'

Christine had stepped back too, the distance between the Howards, Francis St Cartmail, Daniel and her widening by the second. Further away others began to take note of the emotion and the exchanges, a whisper of question circling the room.

'Could I t-talk with you…alone?' Amethyst needed to get away from here, to get outside. Her breathing was strange and the world was beginning to waver. Shock, she thought, and guilt. Every single part of her felt torn.

But Daniel did not move. Two seconds and then three. Both Lucien and Francis on either side of him looked at her strangely, an immobile trio of disbelief mixed with disdain.

'I n-need to explain.' The lies. The omissions. She swallowed and thought she might be sick, here in the grand ballroom of the *ton*, all over her golden foolish dress. 'Please.'

Daniel finally stepped towards her, but he said nothing as he took her arm, a passage of empty space opening as they made their way to the staircase and then down it. Amethyst tried her best not to meet one single person's glance as they went, though she could hear the undercurrents of disparagement all around.

'Trade, of course.' 'Blood will always tell.' 'To think she imagined to hide a husband.'

It was over. Everything. She should have explained to him before now. Lies upon lies upon lies and this is where it got you. Here. The complete disintegration of her name and her character and the derision of the *ton*.

Taking their cloaks and hats from the butler, Daniel strode out to hail his carriage. Any contact had long since gone and he made no effort at all to meet her eyes or to talk.

'There are th-things you need to...'

'Wait until we are alone.' The quiet cold indifference in his voice was far worse than any anger.

A minute later his horses were moving, much faster than she liked, racing towards Grosvenor Square, careening around the corners of the dark London streets.

'Now perhaps you might tell me the truth. Were Lady Mackay's accusations about your marriage to Whitely false or not?'

'It was not as you think...and it was never...' Her attention was caught by the speed the carriage was gaining, fast, much faster than she was comfortable with. The old fear came at her out of nowhere, robbing breath and sense as she lunged for the door handle, peeling her gloves off and keening.

'God.' The Earl's voice came through a melted screen of light. 'What the hell is wrong with you now?'

His discarded cane was in her hand without conscious thought, smooth and warm as she belted the roof as hard as she could, once and then twice before he snatched it away.

'Are you crazy?'

'Too…fast.' Mouthed now as she could not even whisper the words. The carriage would turn over as it had before, she could feel the wheels leaving the ground and lurching sideways. Her heartbeat made her head ache and the old sweat of fear broke out all over her. Then all she knew was a spiralling fog, like snow at night and cold, tunnelling in. She did not try to fight the darkness.

Chapter Seven

They were at Dunstan House and the curtains across the French doors of her room were billowing wide. Like the sails of the Cameron ships on the wind as they raced for the Americas, cargos laden and a blue horizon seen in every direction.

Her father sat in a chair reading, his glasses perched on his nose and a bright floral cushion on his lap. Amethyst's mind searched for an answer as to why they were here and why she was in bed at this time of the day, half a dozen vials of medicine lined up on the table beside her.

Of a sudden the room spun in small and rapid circles, making her blink. Squinting, she reached out, hoping to find balance. Something was not right just beyond thought, the time, the place or the company.

'Papa.' The word was thick in the dryness of her mouth, but her movements had alerted him and, dropping the book on the floor, he reached over to take her hand.

'How do you feel?'

Daniel. He was gone. The ball. Gerald. The wild ride in the carriage home. Too fast.

'How long…since the ball?'

'Three days. This is the first time you have known me.'

'Only…you…here?' Her eyes perused the corners of her chamber, searching. When her father nodded Amethyst allowed the heaviness of her lids to close and she slept.

She knew she was calling his name in the dark and through the night. But Daniel Wylde, the sixth Earl of Montcliffe, would not come because he no longer trusted her, no longer cared.

A cold compress was pressed to her forehead and she touched her father's hand.

'Tired.' She could barely keep her eyes open. 'I feel so tired.'

'Then I will stay with you until you sleep and when you wake up again I shall still be beside you.'

His words were quietly spoken, yet were so

very genuine. She could not remember a time when her father had let her down or failed her. 'I love you, Papa. You have always been here.'

'And I always will be, my jewel. Don't worry. Everything will turn out just exactly as it should, I swear that it will.'

The dizziness was back, hovering at a distance, but closing in. She needed him to know something, but it was hard to think what it was now.

'Daniel?'

'Shush.'

'He makes me…happy.'

The tears fell of their own accord, welling in her eyes and running warm across her cheeks.

'And now…I have lost…him.'

'No.' All the reassurance in the world in that one simple word and as she fell back into sleep she smiled.

The next time she awoke it was dark and two candles on the mantelpiece laid a circle of light across the bed, the white of the counterpane so bright it hurt her eyes to look at. Holding up a hand to dim it, she was surprised by a small cut on her wrist, the blood around the wound dried and powdered. Her father was still beside her, in different clothes now and without the book.

'They bled you. The doctors. I asked them if it was truly necessary but the humours are tricky things, they said, and the melancholy needed to be released from your body.'

Her father looked both exhausted and worried.

'Lord Montcliffe?'

'He left as soon as he brought you home from the Herringworth ball and I haven't heard from him since.'

'Did he tell you…anything?'

He shook his head. 'Maisie and Mick were delivered the next morning and I brought you here the day after that.'

'I see.' And she did. Charlotte Mackay's accusations played on her memory as did the speed of the carriage as Daniel had taken her home. She had acted appallingly, but high emotion, guilt, shame, shock and fright had played their parts, too.

'The doctor administered laudanum to calm you down, my dear, but I do not think it agreed with you. I stopped the dosage the day before yesterday.'

That was why she felt nauseous then and

slightly removed from the world. Her mouth was so parched she could barely swallow but all she could think about was the sense of betrayal in Daniel's pale green eyes.

And the hurt.

The sick feeling in her stomach worsened. He must think her mad and deceitful, a woman who held no regard for honesty or manners; the wife of a man at the centre of a scandal that had rocked all of London. The kiss they had shared came back with full force: a moment in her life she would never forget, a gift of what it might be like to be with a man whom you truly loved.

She turned her face into the pillow and sobbed.

Daniel knew what the lawyer would say. He knew it before the legal retainer even opened his mouth and began to speak.

'I am acting on behalf of the Honourable Reginald Goldsmith. He has instructed me to call in the loan your brother took out against your family estate and he would like the sum paid back in full by the end of this month.'

'I see.'

Smythe shook his head and lifted a yellowing page. 'I am afraid you do not, my lord. The sum is enormous.' Turning the document so that it could be read with more ease, Daniel was stunned.

Five thousand pounds. A king's ransom. So much more than he'd imagined Nigel to have gambled; a fortune that he had no way of getting his hands upon now that Amethyst Cameron had disappeared into the countryside with her father.

'Is there any way I could stretch out the payments?'

'Perhaps for a few months if you were lucky.'

'But no more?'

The lawyer shook his head. 'My client is taking ship to the Americas in twelve weeks because his only daughter has settled in Boston. He wants a clean break and he is more than hopeful that the debts should be discharged before he goes. *Completely discharged*,' he emphasised the words again and wiped his brow. 'Is there a problem with this, Lord Montcliffe?'

'No.' The glint in Smythe's eyes was full of conjecture.

'Your marriage to Miss Cameron should help. I have heard that the family is extremely wealthy. Timber, is it not?'

Daniel stood. He did not wish to hear any

conjecture on his own personal life from a man for whom the words 'appropriate' or 'confidential' appeared to mean nothing. Taking his leave, he was glad Smythe did not engage in further conversation.

He walked along the river in a light rain, the water winding along with him, full of the noise and movement of commerce. Perhaps one of the Cameron ships was docking at this moment, ready to be discharged of its heavy cargo.

Amethyst Cameron.

He no longer knew what to make of her, the shifts of emotion exhausting. He had deposited her at home with her father after the ball and left immediately, her behaviour in the carriage so very deranged and Charlotte's truths still ringing in his ears. The next morning he had sent back the greys. Even to save Montcliffe he could not be for ever tied to a mad and lying wife.

Gerald Whitely, at least, was dead. He had found out that through an investigator he had employed to make sense of it all. But still the whole ending had been maudlin and awkward.

Swearing, he conjured up her face on the night of the ball, her lightened hair showing up the velvet gold in her eyes. Beautiful and crazy. He had not heard a word from the Camerons since and on enquiry found that they had packed up the London town house and headed for their country estate of Dunstan House somewhere up north.

Good riddance, he should have thought, the whole episode so public and brutal. A lucky escape from a woman who was both deceitful and unstable. Yet underneath other thoughts lingered. Amethyst's thinness. The way she smiled. The dimples that dented her cheeks and the careful diction of her words.

He had not made a public statement about anything though the *ton* was, of course, abuzz with the happenings. His mother had caught him in the breakfast room that very morning and made her opinions quite clear.

'From what I have heard you are well shot of Mrs Whitely, Daniel, and you can now concentrate on the search for a far more suitable match. The Earl of Denbeigh's wife, Lady Denbeigh, has been most direct with her wishes for her daughter's future. From all accounts the young lady appears to be a well brought-up, softly spoken girl with an admirable fashion sense. Trade needs to marry trade and those from the *ton* should find a partner within the same ranks. It is these unwritten laws of society that keeps it all working, you see, and if you seek to change it for whatever reason there are always complications and sordid ones at that.'

She twirled the end of a light-brown curl around her finger. 'Your man said you no longer have the greys stabled here in London. Are they at Montcliffe?'

'No. I sent them back to the Camerons. They were part of the wedding settlement.'

'But I had heard that they were worth a fortune.'

'They are.'

'Then I should have kept them if I were you. It would have been some payment for all the humiliation we have suffered since.'

The loud shout of a street pedlar brought Daniel back into the moment, an unkempt fellow playing a wooden flute and touting for a few pennies as he finished. Digging into his pocket, he dropped in an offering.

How the hell could he rescue Montcliffe? The edges of his world were flattening out and he was in danger of falling off the end of it unless he could come up with something.

A pawnshop sign opposite caught his attention and, checking to see that no conveyance was bearing down upon him, he walked across the road towards it, pulling off the heavy gold signet ring from his little finger as he went.

'I think you should send back the greys, Papa. Lord Montcliffe can't wish for the agreements to continue as they were, not after...what has happened, but we do need to ensure his discretion.'

Amethyst finally felt better today and had dressed to come down to the dinner table with her father, who watched her with a growing frown upon his face.

'You won't fight for your reputation, then, or for Lord Montcliffe?'

'He was never mine to fight for, Papa. Surely you can see that?'

'The first man who has made you live again and smile again and you give him up on a sigh? Your mother would have been disappointed in you.'

'Why? Because I can understand that in the distaste of the *ton* lies a way to complete devastation? Daniel Wylde wanted me as little as Whitely did. The pair of greys arrived from him before a new day had dawned properly. Even Gerald gave me a few months.'

'A few months of hell.' Robert stood, his voice louder than she had ever heard it, 'and the scars to prove it. The worst thing about it all was that I could do nothing as Whitely systematically wore you down into a daughter I didn't recognise any more. After him you looked over your shoulder with a fear of life, love and happiness.'

He held up his hand as she went to speak. 'Montcliffe gave you back something whether you admit it or not, Amethyst. For the first time in a long while you have seemed…happy. You took risks, you lived.'

She began to laugh because anything else was too awful to contemplate. 'I agreed to the terms because I thought that was what you wanted, Papa. The doctor said you needed to be relaxed and rested if you were to survive your failing health and you have looked more robust since.'

'I do not think your agreement to marry him was all about me, my dear. You called for Daniel Wylde when you were sick, again and again, and you begged for him to come back.'

'It was the laudanum.'

'No, it was the truth.'

'What are you trying to say, Papa?'

'That the Earl was the best thing that has happened to you in a long time and if you don't do anything to make him understand the situation as you know it you will never be accepted into polite society again. That really would kill me.'

A gathering dread made her feel cold.

'We will introduce better conditions.' Her father's voice held no question as he continued on.

'Conditions?'

'A year of marriage and fifteen thousand pounds every four weeks and then a lump sum at the end.'

She shook her head. 'No more, Papa. We'll simply stay here at Dunstan House. I never need to return to London again.'

'Hiding, then? Like your hands in the gloves and your hair beneath the wig. You're twenty-six, Amethyst, soon to be twenty-seven, and there are not too many of the good years to go. Child-bearing years, the chance of a family and of happiness is dwindling with each and every successive month you tarry. Even now—'

She stopped him. 'I am not an old maid yet.'

'But you might be if you are not careful. Then what would Susannah have to say? Flourishing, she instructed. Make our daughter flourish, were the last words she ever said to me. If you have your way of things there will be no chance of that.'

'So you are saying?'

'That the marriage between you and Daniel Wylde, the Earl of Montcliffe, goes ahead.'

'No.'

'The marriage goes ahead and you show Montcliffe exactly who you are. You tell him the truth about Whitely and the way he used you and hurt you.'

'No, I can't do that.'

'Then I will call in each and every debt his estate owes and ruin him. Is that what you want?'

'I don't believe you are saying these things, Papa.' Horror stripped her words back to a whisper.

'If you tell me you have absolutely no feelings for Lord Daniel Wylde, I will stop. All of this. We will simply leave England and head… anywhere. But you must also remember that there is every good chance according to the best of London's specialists that you will soon be completely alone and without my support.'

She was silent. She tried to speak, she did, from the well of sense and logic and reason she knew was inside her, but the words just would not come.

Relief passed into the lines of her father's face. 'Very well. I shall send Montcliffe a message tomorrow outlining the new conditions, Amethyst. If I have not heard back from him by the end of the week, I will go down to London myself and visit him. I do not think he is a person who would break his word on keeping the silence of our demands and I also know that Goldsmith will be calling in his own debts, too.'

'My God.'

'Are we in agreement, then?'

She could imagine Daniel receiving both her father's and Goldsmith's demands all in the same month. Pale green eyes rose in memory, the golden shards warm with humour at the ball and then icy with distaste in the carriage.

Once he had admired her, she could tell that he had. Once he had trusted her and lauded her honesty and truth. Once he had kissed her, sensuously, expertly, so that the blood in her temple had pounded in an unending and heavy din. More. More. More.

That was the worst of it. She had pressed her body back against his own as they had danced and known the hard outline of his sex. She had felt his breath mingle with hers, life-giving and wonderful, his lips so close, his smile just for her, the light of the chandeliers falling in quiet patterns across them, magical and bliss filled.

Oh, how he must be laughing now.

Crazy, deceitful Amethyst Cameron, trading her way into a betrothal that he did not wish for and refusing to let him go.

If she had any sense left, she would instruct her father not to take things further, then simply accept what had happened and move on.

To what? To where?

The quandary bewildered her. Without the Camerons' money Daniel would have to sell Montcliffe Manor and she knew him well enough to understand that would be something he would hate to do. Marriage, then, to another heiress, another woman who might sweeten the pot with gold and property. And a hasty one at that given the timings.

Nay, she might still be the best of all evils if she threw down her cards in the right order and gave him space to play it out. Marriage was like business, after all, and both parties had to feel they had made a good deal or things quickly went sour.

'I will agree to try again, Papa, but this time I will write my own conditions.'

'Very well.' The smile in his eyes was bountiful.

Taking a sheet of paper from an armoire on one side of the room, she proceeded to do just that.

Daniel could not believe what he was reading. The Camerons' lawyer, Alfred Middlemarch, on the other side of the table sat very still, no expression on his face, a man used to the strange and fickle ways of the very rich.

'And they want me to sign this today?'

'They do, my lord, and most generous Mr Robert Cameron has been, there is no doubt on that. I do not think he wishes to draw out the procedure, so to speak, but wants a quick and expeditious process so that all concerned might move on in the right direction with their lives.'

The right direction?

Goldsmith's lawyer had been to see him again yesterday with his own amended set of demands. Four weeks now and no longer the stated twelve to repay the debt. A coincidence? Daniel thought not. Other debtors, too, had foreclosed as word had spread of the poor financial status of the Wyldes. He could barely keep up with the sums mooted or the spiralling escalation of debt.

'There is also a page of further conditions that Miss Cameron herself has penned. She asked me to give them to you under strict confidence and made me promise to reiterate that you were not to let anyone else know of them. Including myself. She has made me promise that I shall burn the paper as soon as you leave unless you wish to take it with you.'

The missive was sealed, the red wax engraved with the letter 'C', two yellow ribbons splayed out beneath it.

Pulling on the tabs Daniel brought the sheet into the light. The hand was neat and small, flourishes of fancy every so often at the end of a sentence.

If you are reading this I want you to know how sorry I am for all that has happened. It was not meant to be this way.

Your family's well-being is as important to you as my father's happiness is to me, so if this marriage is to go ahead I propose that:

You can build up a stable of breeding

horses at the Dunstan stables that would be unlike anything else seen in England.

You have carte blanche *on buying the livestock.*

We will have as little to do with each other's daily lives as you wish for.

My personal fortune will be at your disposal to ensure the future of the Montcliffe lineage and property as well as that of Dunstan House.

Yours sincerely
Amethyst Amelia Cameron

'Damn.' He muttered the word beneath his breath and the man opposite looked up.

'I hope it is to your liking, my lord.' The expressionless face of Middlemarch neither softened nor hardened. 'Will you take it with you or shall I burn it?'

'I will keep it.'

'Very well. I do not wish to hurry you along, Lord Montcliffe, but…'

'You are a busy man.'

'Exactly. The Camerons have always been good clients and honest people. Their payments are regular and prompt and in all my years of working with Mr Robert Cameron I have seldom heard one bad word against him, professionally or personally.'

The Montcliffe family lawyer chose that point to turn from the window. Mr Athol Bailey was of the old school of law, but had allowed the Cameron's legal representative to outline the terms of the agreement mooted in his office. For his own benefit Daniel thought, but also as a means to an end. The Montcliffe fortune was in danger of collapsing completely and the severity of the problem was not going to just go away. Bailey spoke now as he rounded the desk to sit in a leather chair to one side of it.

'The word about town, Lord Montcliffe, is that other parties hold several loans against the Montcliffe estate and they are interested in settling them quickly. Lord Greyton's representative, for example, is a colleague of mine and, whilst I hope I do not speak out of turn, I would say that the general opinion is that you are on the verge of bankruptcy. As your family retainer, my lord, and given the expenses that your mother incurs in her daily and general life, I would advise you to reflect very carefully about an offer that could only be conducive to the financial well-being of the Wyldes from now on and into the future.'

'I see.'

For the first time that morning Bailey smiled and, looking over at the Cameron's lawyer, Daniel spoke. 'Will you take a message back for me? I would require an answer as soon as possible.'

'Of course.'

'Could you tell the Camerons that I agree to their proposals, but the small wedding will be held at Montcliffe Manor. I want only my bride and her father to be in attendance. No one else.'

'Certainly, my lord.'

'Could you also tell Miss Cameron that I shall be sending her a bill for the damage incurred to the roof of my carriage whilst she was under the influence of her fit of madness.'

'Indeed, my lord.' Middlemarch's countenance did not falter as he handed over one of his inked quills. 'Just here, if you may.' He waited until the deed was signed before flipping over to another. 'And here.'

Finally the old lawyer stood, depositing the documents into a well-worn leather briefcase. 'I consider my business done and I would like to thank you both for allowing me the time and place to present this agreement. I hope you are as happy with the outcome as I know my clients shall be, Lord Montcliffe, and I wish you the very best for the future.'

Ten minutes later Daniel was back on the street and his mood was as black as the clouds he could see amassing over to the west. He had been played like a fish on the line, the bait of his own demise as imminent as the Camerons would know it to be. Until this past week he had not had one single debt of his brother's presented to him. Did Robert Cameron have some dealings there as well to force his hand and hurry things up?

But why would he do so? Surely a dozen other down-on-their-luck lords could be cajoled into a union with Miss Amethyst Cameron and with far more ease, even given the scandalous nature of her first husband's business.

His mind went back to the carriage ride home. She had acted like a crazed woman, with little sense or reasonableness, her shrill cries still ringing in his ears. He had never met another like her, that was the trouble, one part innocent and the other part as deceptive as hell. She was her father's daughter on the one hand and her own particular mix of madness on the other.

Yet he had signed on the dotted line. For his mother and his sisters and a grandfather who barely knew the time of day.

'More fool me,' he muttered, pleased to see his town house materialise before him and also the possibility of a stiff drink. His lineage would stay safe and Montcliffe Manor would not need to be sold. Such protections would have to be enough. The dull ache in his thigh mirrored the pain in his head.

Charlotte Mackay arrived on his doorstep just as he did and this time there was no mother or brother anywhere in sight.

'Might I come in just for a moment, Daniel? I realise that I am hardly the person you wish to see, but I would appreciate at least a moment or two of your time.'

Today she was dressed in a woollen cloak with the buttons done up tightly to her neck. With a quick nod he showed her through to his library, but he did not sit down as he waited for an explanation as to why she had come.

'I am more than sorry for the scene at the Herringworth ball. I have been trying to get up the courage to allow explanation, but it has been hard.' Swallowing she looked at him.

'The allotted period of mourning society

deems appropriate for a bereaved widow has been most…difficult and it is only in the past month that I have been allowed to enjoy my life again. As a result of everything I have come to the conclusion that a year of black clothes and dour conversation shows not only the nonsense of marriage but also my unsuitability to such a state.'

'In what way?' For the life of him he could not understand why she should be telling him this.

Her right forefinger tucked an errant golden curl up into the folds of her hat as she gave him answer. 'I am committed to enjoying every single moment I have left to me, Daniel. After Spenser I saw that sometimes bad things can happen.' Shaking her head, she went on, drawing herself up a little. 'Your finances are in a poor state. I have heard that from many people and your brother's problems at the card table are no longer a secret. As my own bank accounts are most healthy I thought perhaps as a friend I could offer you a way out of the mess you now find yourself in.'

He knew what was coming and he tried to stop her by holding up his hand, but she took little notice of the gesture.

'I will pay off some of your debts in exchange for you and I becoming lovers again. I have missed you and I made a huge mistake when Spenser offered for my hand. But now there is an opportunity for us…'

'No.' He could say it in no other way than that.

'No?'

'Thank you, but I cannot take you up on the offer, Charlotte.'

'Because you are angry at me for ruining your chances with Mrs Whitely?'

At that he laughed. 'Hardly.'

'Then why?'

He took his time in answering. 'Spenser was an only child and the last of his family line. I have heard it said that his parents want you to reside with them in Scotland in return for the large sums of money they have bestowed upon you and which you accepted on your husband's death. It seems Spenser Mackay's mother thinks of you as a daughter?'

'You sound like my mother, Daniel, and I do not want to hear this.' Moving closer, she brought her fingers along the line of his cheek. 'Scotland is full of sad memories for me and I want to feel again what I did, with you, in your arms, before it all went wrong.'

Once he might have been flattered by the offer she had just made him, but now all he could think about was the chaos of their past. 'I think, Charlotte, that the time for us has gone.'

'Kiss me then and tell me that afterwards.'

She did not wait for him to move, but pressed herself up against him, her lips brushing along his own, warm and full and remembered. The same smell of gardenias and the same feel of softness.

Shaking his head, he placed both hands on her shoulders and moved her away. Carefully. The clock in the corner boomed out the hour of three and apart from the sound of its heavy ticking there was silence in the room.

'You won't allow me in because of your brother? Nigel was a…dalliance. I knew as soon as we had slept together it was a mistake.'

He tried to smother the anger that he could feel building. 'If it was not Nigel, then it would have been someone else, Charlotte, and by then I did not care enough anyway.'

'You are refusing me?'

'I am.'

'But I love you, Daniel. I have always loved

you.' She was crying now, the tears running down her cheeks. 'You were distant at the end of…us. If you had been more attentive, none of this would ever have happened. But we can change it and with only a little effort we could again be—'

'Stop. The time for regrets is past and you have duties now to Spenser Mackay's family and to your own.'

Rather than placating her, this line of argument made her wail louder. 'Then both of us have lost and all for nothing, and you will regret this, I know that you will.'

Gathering up her reticule, she opened the door, his man coming forward immediately to show her out. When she was gone Daniel crossed to his desk and sat down. The letter he had received at his lawyer's today rustled and he brought the sheet from his pocket. Amethyst's demands juxtaposed against those of Charlotte's made him feel his life was taking a less-than-salutary course.

Lucien's voice in the corridor had him flicking the missive into a drawer as he waited for his friend to come into the room.

'Tell me that was not Lady Charlotte Mackay in the carriage I just saw pulling away, Daniel, for I thought that affair was long since over.' As he dropped into the leather chair nearest the desk he reached out for the decanter, upturning a clean glass and pouring a generous libation.

'It isn't what you think. We are friends.' As he said it he wondered if Charlotte and he were even that.

'She's poison, damn it. She betrayed you with Nigel and she could so easily do so again.'

'I know.'

'Do you?'

'Lady Mackay will be returning to Scotland to live. She just came to say goodbye.'

'She still loves you. You can see it in her eyes. My guess is that she came to beg forgiveness as she tried to inveigle her way back into your bed with money and sex. The cloak she wore was a surprise though, buttoned as it was to the neck. Not her usual style.'

Daniel finished his drink before he spoke. 'Let it go, Luce. There is no purpose in flogging the past.'

'Maybe not, but your present difficulties can be laid squarely at the feet of Lady Mackay and rumour has it that Goldsmith is calling in his loan. Can you pay him?'

Daniel shook his head, helping himself to

more of the same smooth wine. 'There are others as well. Nigel was busier than I had thought.'

'Pity Amethyst Cameron turned out to be such a duplicitous liar. I liked her before that. Francis told me to tell you that you should follow him to America. By his accounts there is a fortune to be made there.'

'I don't have enough time left to find it.'

'Your mother?'

'Is finally terrified. In the past few days and for the first time ever she is cursing Nigel to a most uncomfortable afterlife.'

'At least she is recognising he is the architect of much of the Montcliffe misfortune. I could sell Cosgrove Hall. It is mine outright to do as I want with and it should fetch something even in its dilapidated state. At least the land around is arable.'

Daniel smiled. 'I thank you for that, Luce, but it would hardly cover the first loan that was presented.'

'Marry a girl whose family is flush, then, a young debutante who'd fall in love with you in a second. That would do the trick.'

'I think any chaperone would be hurrying such prospects away from me. There is a big difference in thinking a family on the verge of ruin and the knowing of it. Besides, I am too jaded to be tiptoeing around such innocence.'

And he was, Daniel thought in surprise. Even the idea of such a bride made him feel… nervous. He was thirty-four next birthday and he felt older than that again. He didn't want a woman he could hardly speak to or one who would be running home to her mother every time the going got tough. Which it would. His leg was aching tonight and he knew very soon he'd need to get a surgeon to look at it properly.

'Did you find out anything more of Gerald Whitely then? You mentioned that you were looking into it the last time we met.'

Daniel nodded. 'He died in the bed of a prostitute, it seems. Two shots to the head and no one ever held accountable. His crooked schemes of business were apparently funded by the Camerons' money.'

Lucien swore. One of the riper expressions remembered from army life.

'My thoughts exactly.'

'I can't see Miss Cameron being enamoured with someone of that ilk even after all that has happened and I am sure she could not have condoned his scandalous get-rich deals, either. As an impartial viewer I would also like to say that for the first time in a long while you seemed happy when you were with her.'

The words rang in Daniel's head like a death knell as he struggled to change the subject to something lighter. He hadn't been happy in so long, that was the problem. He couldn't remember a time when he had truly laughed or enjoyed something just for the fun of it.

A band of yellow roses in golden curls came to mind, and lips that turned up at each end even when she did not smile. After Nigel and Charlotte, honesty was the yardstick he had measured people by and Amethyst Cameron had failed that test miserably in the end.

If the Camerons sent back an agreement to his terms, would he still go through with it, knowing all that he did? Was Montcliffe Manor worth such a sacrifice?

Charlotte's presence today had unsettled him, but so had his mother's constant tears. The carrot of building up his own breeding stable also sat at the back of his mind. With luck and good management he could begin to prosper and in a couple of years he might be able to pay back much of the debt. Amethyst had come to him stipulating her own terms, after all, so she would not be clinging on to something unsustainable either.

A marriage of convenience and with many of the terms in his favour? He could build up his breeding stock and begin again. A new life with the freedom of money and time. But even that prospect failed to allow him any renewed hopefulness and his shattered right thigh hurt like hell.

Chapter Eight

She would be married in an hour. Again. In a house she had no notion of and in a dress hurriedly made, with little interest on her part for the end result.

She looked terrible, that much she could see, her eyes red and swollen and the eczema that had a tendency to appear when she was stressed staining her cheeks and the soft skin beneath her mouth.

A blemished bride.

An unwanted bride.

A second-hand bride.

A bride who would stand at the altar only because of a series of conditions that would allow her husband a separate life apart from hers. Montcliffe had signed such stipulations in haste, hadn't he, the avenues of finding a solution to his own problems closing in.

Unlocking the golden cross that she wore around her neck, she laid it down on the bedside table.

'I do not want you to be a part of this charade, Mama.' Her neck seemed empty without the chain, though today her mother felt close.

Susannah Cameron had been a redhead, with a freckled skin and a verve for life that was uncompromising. She had risked the small loan her father had bequeathed to her when he had died as a down payment for the first of Robert's boats. The best spend of my life, she had said to Robert again and again as Amethyst had grown, the love her parents shared a constant and joyous source of wonderment.

So different from this marriage, the ghost of Gerald Whitely surfacing in threat. 'Daniel Wylde will turn out just like me,' some spectral voice whispered. 'The very same, you just wait, for you are cursed and marked.'

Swallowing, she turned away from the mirror. Her maid had helped her to dress, but had gone now to let those downstairs know that she was ready. Amethyst thought her hair looked nothing like it had when Lady Christine had threaded it with roses. Rather it was spiked and ill shaped, the golden band of her mother's she had insisted on wearing seeming as out of kilter as her dress.

Pure white. She wondered if she should have worn the colour, but the seamstress had already begun on it when the thought occurred and so she had taken the path of least resistance and left it as it was. At least the veil would hide some of her defects. With care she pulled the gauze across her face and smiled, glad of the opaqueness and privacy.

A few moments later she entered the downstairs salon at Montcliffe, a room of huge proportion and elegance, though sparsely furnished.

Lord Daniel Wylde was there, of course, and her father. Beside them stood the minister and an older woman.

Four people; two of whom she did not know. The conditions he had insisted upon. A small marriage. Uncelebrated. Forgettable.

'We shall repair to the chapel for the ceremony.' Daniel's voice, but he neither took her hand nor looked at her directly, leaving it to her father to accompany her. The room appeared otherworldly through the gauze.

'You look lovely, my dear,' Robert said beneath his breath, and for the first time that day she smiled.

'I think even you know that that is a lie, Papa.'

The house had been a revelation when she had first seen it the day before. It was huge for one thing and sombre for another. Not a house one would feel at home in, she had thought, and wondered at what sort of a childhood the manor might have provided for a young Daniel. Everything looked old and the faded spaces on the walls alluded to another long-ago time when Montcliffe Manor must have been magnificent.

The Earl had met them briefly here yesterday, outlining the planned ceremony in formal tones and then leaving. The same butler she remembered from the London town house had shown them to their rooms on the first storey and the dark furniture in each was as Spartan as the rest of the place.

She had not seen him since. Today he looked taller and as forbidding as his house. She wondered if she had truly ever known him, a stranger with whom she had shared a kiss.

The minister stood at the pulpit and gestured for them to come before him.

'Who gives this woman in marriage?' he asked gravely.

'I do.' Robert's voice was guarded, as if he

too wondered if they had not made an enormous mistake.

And then her arm was threaded with that of Daniel's, superfine beneath her fingers and the outline of heavy muscle under the fabric.

Delivered.

Into a union that neither of them looked forward to and married under the solemn words of promise. Little words that meant both everything and nothing.

A ring was slipped on to the third finger of her left hand, the huge diamond glinting in the light and pulling at her skin.

'I now pronounce you man and wife.'

And it was over, the older lady signing beneath their names, a legal witness along with her father to the nuptials.

Her husband's full name was Daniel George Alexander Wylde. Something else she had not known about him.

Robert took her hand as she stepped back, his glance warm when he looked at the ring. 'A substantial diamond,' he said, and she knew that there were things he did not know about her either. The day was threaded with strangeness and juxtaposition. When Amethyst glanced up she saw Daniel watching her, his pale eyes hooded.

The wedding breakfast was set up in the blue salon to one end of the house and, once they were all seated, an awkwardness overcame everything. At least the minister was talking, his words running into each other in a never-ending stream. Otherwise there might have been silence as each player in this travesty sought their place within it.

A headache burned into her temples, the laudanum still in her system somewhere and making itself felt. Her father looked worried and thin, none of the certainty that had been there in the days leading up to this moment evident. She had no clue at all about Daniel's frame of mind because an implacable mask crossed his face and his eyes were a flat distant green.

The food was lovely, a light soup and then chicken and beef with an array of sauces and roasted vegetables. A cake was presented, too, and it sat on the end of the table couched in a feigned joviality, two figures carved in icing upon it, their arms entwined around each other.

Amethyst drank deeply from her wine glass, something she seldom did, but the velvet-smooth red banished some of her worries. Then her groom stood to propose a toast.

'To my bride. May this union be kind to us both.'

The hollow thud of her heart made her feel sick and, as she lifted her hand to push back a falling curl, the diamond ring sliced a scratch right across her cheek. Her father used a snowy-white napkin to wipe away the blood.

How he hated this.

His new wife looked scared and lost, but he was too angry to understand anything other than retribution. Symbols. The blood, the diamond, the cake with its ridiculous illusion of happiness and joy. He felt none of it. Too few people at the table, too many lies left unsaid.

This wedding was a parody and the guest list reflected the fact. He had not told Lucien or Francis that he was getting married and his own family thought he had gone to Montcliffe Manor to recover from the events at the Herringworth ball. Recover? Like he had after La Corunna? In their ignorance he saw just how little they knew about him.

Robert Cameron was looking disappointed rather than furious and that annoyed him further. He had been coerced into this whole situation by a master. The timber merchant could not expect him to enjoy it.

The huge diamond on his wife's finger was patently wrong and he saw now that part of the gold clasp had worn free from the stone it held. It had hurt her.

Yesterday he might have smiled at such a travesty, but today the short spikiness of her hair pulled at him somehow. She had threaded a gold headband through the curls in an effort to emulate what Christine Howard had once done, but it only added a poignant awkwardness and the scars on her wrist above the gaudy diamond were reddened. Like her face.

When he had raised the veil after the vows all he saw was skin that was rough and raw, her dark eyes taking in the fact that he was seeing her at her very worst.

But even like that she looked beautiful to him. He ground his teeth in rage.

Her father was speaking now to the small and mismatched group around the table, thin lines of sickness etched into his face.

'I have always called Amethyst "my jewel" and I hope in the coming years you might see the truth in these words for yourself, Lord

Montcliffe.' He raised his glass and toasted. 'To Lord and Lady Montcliffe. May their union be blessed with love and laughter.'

At least he had not intimated heirs. Breathing out, Daniel looked at the fob at his waist. Another few minutes and this would all be over.

Her groom kept checking the time, five minutes and then ten. The food was tasty and the conversation around the table increasingly more congenial, but he did not join in the talk and neither did she, the minister and her father doing most of it.

Unexpectedly the older woman next to her leant over and squeezed her hand. 'I am Julia McBeth and when I was married I wondered what I was doing, but my Henry was the sweetest man a bride could want. Daniel Wylde is like that too, underneath. He is kind and good.'

She spoke quietly, but in her eyes there was a genuine concern.

'I was the Earl's governess when he was young. His mother was not the sort of woman who took to children easily, you understand, so the two boys became like the sons I could never have myself. I am a distant cousin from a branch of the family that invested unwisely, so the position here was a godsend at the time, and the boys made everything bearable. I left Montcliffe Manor when Nigel and Daniel were sent up to school, but kept in good contact with the boys afterwards.'

'You must miss Nigel, then?'

'Oh, I do, but he always needed his younger brother to keep him…stable. When Daniel went off to the Peninsular Campaign with General Moore I think Nigel lost his direction and could not get it back.

'So he died before my husband returned?'

'Just a day or so after, actually.' The frown across her forehead alluded to something more, but Amethyst did not wish to ask about it. 'My husband passed away three years ago and although I had been away from Montcliffe for a very long time Lord Montcliffe asked me back to stay. A goodness, that, for I had nowhere else to go and I think he knew it.'

'Do his mother and sisters ever come here?'

'The Countess is a city woman. I doubt she has ever enjoyed the place and only a small handful of staff has been kept on which would not suit her at all. Certainly even as a young mother Lady Montcliffe left for London at the drop of a hat and for very long periods of time.'

'Then it is most appropriate that you are here today, Mrs McBeth.'

'Julia. Everyone calls me that and if you have need of an ear you know where to find me.'

'Thank you.' A slight happiness came through all the strange uncertainty as she was given a glimpse of the younger Daniel. A leader and kind with it. The sort of man that Gerald had never been.

When the meal finally came to an end the Earl of Montcliffe stood.

'Might I have a word with you in private in the library, my lady?' My lady? She was that to him now? So formal. So very polite.

'Of course.'

She followed him down a dark corridor that opened up into a large and light room, a garden off to one side with double doors for access. Books lined each end, all leather-bound and well ordered.

Here was another thing then that she had discovered about him. He read.

'Your lawyer gave me your handwritten note outlining the demands of this marriage. A marriage in name only, I am presuming, given your edict for separate lives.'

Did he want more? Looking up, she saw he did not.

'For appearances' sake would you be happy to inhabit the adjoining chamber to my own whilst here at Montcliffe Manor? It might stop any gossip that I would not wish to engender. The door between us would remain locked, the key on your side.'

She nodded.

'Did your father read the conditions you wrote?'

'He didn't.'

'His seemed to contradict your own.'

'I think he hopes for much more than each of us would wish to give, my lord.'

'Indeed?'

His hand reached out towards her and he tipped her chin up into the light, peering at her injured cheek. 'That should not have happened.' Colouring profusely, she felt the heat of his words roll across her face. 'Did you love Gerald Whitely, Amethyst?'

'No.'

For the only time in that whole day he smiled like he meant it, as he let her go. 'We will stay here at Montcliffe until the day after tomorrow.

Then we shall travel to Dunstan House. Your father will accompany us.'

'You have spoken to him of it?'

'Yes.'

He turned then to the cabinet behind him and, using a key, unlocked a safe that held a long leather box. She saw a profusion of small boxes within, but stayed quiet whilst he opened one container and then the next. Finally he found what he sought and came to stand beside her.

'Give me your left hand.' With trepidation she did so, watching as he carefully removed the ugly diamond ring and replaced it with a delicate deep purple amethyst set in ornately wrought rose gold.

'The clasp on this one won't hurt you.'

Smooth and beautiful, the underlying colours of red and blue glinted in the light of the room. No small worth.

'It is my birthstone.'

'I know.'

She was surprised at this. 'What stone is yours?'

'A diamond for April.'

Without meaning to she laughed and the humour was not lost on him.

'The hardest substance on earth.' He waited for a moment before carrying on. 'Imbued in the folktale is the belief that diamonds promote eternal love.'

A new awareness filled the space around them.

'We barely know each other, but the circumstances that have thrown us together require at least some effort of knowledge. Perhaps if we start here.'

'Here?'

'My parents loathed each other from the moment they married and I do not wish to be the same. Is politeness beyond us, do you think?'

She shook her head.

Her hand was still in his, the warmth of skin comforting and sensual, though after a quick shake he allowed her distance.

'Would you come for a ride with me around the Montcliffe estate this afternoon?'

'In your carriage?'

'I thought after our last jaunt together that you might prefer horseback. The stables here are not quite empty yet.'

When she nodded he leant down to ring the bell and a servant she hadn't seen before appeared immediately.

'Could you show Lady Montcliffe back to her room?' He consulted the same watch she had seen him glance at before. 'Would an hour be enough time for you to be ready?'

'Yes.'

'Then I will see you at the stables at four.'

A slight gesture to his man had him turning. He did not look back as he opened a further door to one end of the library and disappeared from view.

He walked into his brother's chamber after their conversation and sat in the chair before the desk in the untouched room. Nigel was everywhere, in the models of ships that might ply the Atlantic much like Cameron's fleet and in the books of maps that he had treasured in a wayward pile next to his bed. He had barely been in here since his brother's death, but this was a room he had often enjoyed as a youth.

Daniel could not decide which emotion he felt more, love or anger, but they were both closely aligned to the guilt he had never let go of.

He should have been able to save Nigel as he had in their childhood when his brother would ride too fast or lean out too far. Daniel had been younger by eighteen months, but he had always felt older, more in control, and the Earldom had not suited his sibling's temperament.

Responsibility worried Nigel and he began to drink heavily. A week before Daniel left for Europe he had found Charlotte Hughes *déshabillée* in the attic of the stables entwined in the arms of his brother, an identical look of shame and shock on both their faces.

His former lover was no loss whatsoever, but Nigel's betrayal was. Daniel had not sought him out when he left England with his regiment, an action he regretted when a bullet went through his leg in Penasquedo as he tried to shelter Moore from the battle, and regretted again when the fever took him into the realm of pain, heat and hopelessness on the transports home.

Charlotte had long gone north with her rich Scottish beau by the time he returned and his brother had been drawn into the company of a group of men who had forgotten what was good and true and sound about life.

Sometimes Daniel thought he had forgotten, too, but he was fighting to cling on and Amethyst Cameron was a part of that, despite the lies about her dead husband.

After he had begun to recover from the

wound to his thigh from La Corunna he had gone to recuperate at the London town house. His mother and sisters had left to stay with an aunt in Coventry, the sudden shock of the death of Nigel affecting his mother in a way that had made her even more unstable. Hence, when Daniel arrived home from the hospital and in no fit state to travel, his grandfather was the only person left in residence in town.

Harold Heatley-Ward had been a man of few words all of his life, but in the time they were thrown unexpectedly together, he had begun to talk more and Daniel would hobble each night to his grandfather's sitting room.

'Your mother was never an easy woman, Daniel. I blame my wife for spoiling her and allowing her every wish. Sometimes disappointment and frustration can help to build a character's resilience. Janet never had a chance to nurture hers and as an only child was wont to get whatever she favoured.'

He'd produced a large bottle of whisky after the confession, taking the top off it with a sort of quiet excitement.

'The stuff of legend,' he had said. 'Brandy hasn't a heart compared to the best of what Scotland can offer and whilst we are alone with no one to sanction our taste we should enjoy it.'

And they had until well into the following morning.

'Your brother left you a letter, by the way,' his grandfather had confessed at around three o'clock, words slurred. His movements were clumsy, too, as he went to retrieve the missive from a drawer next to his bed. From the drink or from the creeping arthritis, there was no true way to tell.

'Nigel made me swear that I would not give this to you until we were alone. Unseen if you like. From such instructions I have taken it that he did not wish for your mother to read the thing.'

'Have you? Read it, I mean?'

'No. It is sealed.' He handed over the note. 'From Nigel's state of mind when he gave it to me I think I have a fair idea about what it might contain.'

Daniel hadn't known whether to open it up then and there or leave it until later. But, cognisant of his grandfather's worry, he broke the wax.

Daniel,

You always knew what to say and do. You should have been the Earl because I have made an awful hash of it and I don't know which way to turn any more. Now that you are home in England again the Montcliffe estate may have found its saviour.

Seeing you yesterday in London has confirmed my belief that if I wasn't in the world things would be easier for everyone. However, I am sorry for ending it the way that I hope to. A shot to the temple is quick, but unlike you I have always been a coward. I also sincerely hope that any debt I have incurred will die with me. I pray and hope history will record my demise as an accident.

Grandfather has promised to deliver this letter to you when a moment arises where he has you alone. I think he understands me better than anyone. Tomorrow I leave for Montcliffe Manor and I don't mean to come back.

The letter was signed with an N., embellished with two long flicks and underlined.

Closing his eyes against the tilting world, Daniel screwed the paper up in a tight ball and tried to hold in the utter sadness.

'His servant was adamant that the gun went off by mistake as he jumped a fence?' The question in his grandfather's tone was brittle and Daniel passed the missive over and waited until Harold had read it.

'It is not a surprise,' the old man finally said, tears welling in his eyes. 'Nigel took the world too seriously until he started to gamble, then he forgot to think about anything else at all. Your father was afflicted with the same sort of sickness.'

Anger claimed reason at the ease of such an excuse as Daniel stood, trying to control his fury. 'When I was in Spain I saw men fight for their country and die for liberty and loyalty. This sort of death is…wasteful.'

But his grandfather shook his head. 'Be pleased that the same melancholy that took over your brother's mind was not inherent in your own.'

'A coward simply lets go. A braver man might fight.'

'You were the only one of the Wyldes who ever knew how to do that. You escaped, can't you see, with your friends and your school and your unwillingness to belong here in a household that did not understand the importance of family or loyalty or lineage.'

He had never belonged. The thought came quick and true. But neither had Nigel, in the cutthroat tug of war between his parents and the quieter but equally brutal boarding school that they were both finally sent to.

There Daniel had met Lucien and Francis, but Nigel had drifted on the edges of friendships, never quite establishing himself in any particular group.

'Janet would most likely be even more heartbroken if she knew the truth. If we could keep this from her...?'

Harold left the option as a question, and Daniel found himself nodding as he took the confession over to the hearth, struck a tinder and watched the flame catch. Indeed, an accident whilst out hunting was a lot more palatable to explain.

The smoke rose in small curls from the missive, there was a slight flare of flame and then it was gone. Scuffing the ashes with his boot to make sure the damning truth was lost, he turned to his grandfather.

'I am glad Nigel felt he could at least trust you in the end.'

The old man merely nodded his head and bent to watch the last puffs of grey smoke, tears still rolling down both his cheeks.

Montcliffe was a beautiful property, Amethyst thought, the house sitting on a lake and surrounded by sloping meadows and falling to a river that wound through a valley. Everything was green.

'My father and Nigel never really understood the history here at Montcliffe or the beauty of it.'

On top of the same large black stallion he had ridden in London her husband looked… unmatched. Amethyst smiled at the word and his eyebrows rose.

'But you love this place.'

He nodded. 'It's the peace of the country, I suppose, and the silence, though I have not spent as much time here as I would have liked to.'

Each word made her pleased. He was not a man who over-enjoyed the party life, then. Like Gerald.

'And your family?'

'This was my father's heritage. My mother seldom ventures far from the social scene in

Brighton in summer or London over the winter. I doubt she enjoyed it here right from the time she and my father married and my sisters have not either.'

'You are lucky to have so many close relatives.'

When he laughed she wondered if he felt the same, but the sun was on her face and it felt so good to be riding. Here and now, the strained events leading up to their wedding were further afield.

'Did your first husband like horses?'

The bubble popped completely, but she made herself answer.

'I think he felt daunted by any outdoor pursuit.'

'What did he like then?'

Not me.

She wondered what would happen if she just said it, blurted the truth out about how in the end he hated every single thing she stood for. But that honesty was too brutal even for her, and there were things that she would never tell another soul. Staying silent, she did not add all of the sordid, degenerate and shameful facts and there were so very many of them.

'The mistakes of others are not our own,' he said quietly.

She smiled, liking his sentiment, but the tears that sat at the back of her eyes felt close.

'My father has a habit of saying the same.'

'Then it is time you believed it.'

'Papa insists that people come upon the destiny they deserve, but I always thought that was a bit harsh.'

'Why?'

'Sometimes destiny just falls on our heads and squashes us flat.'

He began to laugh. 'If you are referring to yourself, you have never seemed squashed to me.'

Delight ran through her at the compliment and just like that the ache in her body was explained.

She was falling in love with the Earl of Montcliffe. She was. She was allowing herself to believe the fairy tale and ignore all the conditions of what, to him, would be simply a way out of bankruptcy.

He was innately kind—had not Mrs McBeth told her so?—and he was a gentleman reared in the art of manners and comportment. He had asked for civility and she had agreed, so her ridiculous want for more could only embarrass them both.

Already he was looking away, waving to a man who worked in the fields. The late sun gave the Earl's hair dark red lights and when his horse reared to one side he easily controlled it, gentling the stallion with a few well-chosen words.

She had never before been around someone who was as effortlessly certain, the smile on his face breaking the skin around his eyes into lines. Perhaps he was also a man who laughed a lot. She hoped so.

'Your father's pallor seems better here than in the city?'

'That is because his favourite places are the countryside and the ocean, and he thinks the land is beautiful around here.'

'Did you ever go with him to the Americas?'

'When I was younger I did. But then...' She stopped.

'Then?' He looked at her carefully, a slight puzzlement in his eyes.

'I became a different person. I would like to say that the display of histrionics in the carriage was not my finest hour, my lord. The accident that resulted in the loss of my hair came when travelling too fast and now whenever I am inside a conveyance that goes at more than a walking pace, I panic. Normally I am innately sensible and very correct. I like order and regularity and control and seldom let my emotions rule me. My temperament is usually far less emotional and far more calm, if you are able to believe it. After the Herringworth ball the shock of everything made me…unreasonable and I am sorry for my behaviour.'

A shout had them both turning and a man on a horse was coming across the field towards them.

'Smithson is one of the cottars and he wants a word with me. We will have to finish this conversation later, but thank you for the explanation.'

Nodding, she jammed her shaking hands into the divided skirt of her riding attire and hoped Daniel had not seen the racing pulse at her throat.

Chapter Nine

They had an early dinner and it was a simple affair, the leftover meats from the wedding breakfast and a bowl of fruit in season. Mrs Orchard, the housekeeper, had cut up the cake and arranged the pieces carefully on a plate. The same figurines from the wedding now twirled in the middle on their own revolving pedestal. An eternal embrace.

Her father was in a good mood, his appetite the best Amethyst had seen it for months as he helped himself to the food.

'Your man showed me around the stables, Lord Montcliffe, and impressive it was, too. Who built them?' The lilt in his voice was audible.

'My great-grandfather. He was a firm believer in the philosophy that horses need a view to thrive so every stall looks across the lake.'

Robert began to laugh. 'You will find Dunstan House to be nowhere near as attractive, though we can rebuild everything to imitate the style here if that is your wish.'

The conditions of their union came to the table with them, Amethyst thought, all present and accounted for, each one a reminder of the absence of what should have been. She wished her father might just leave it at that, but as he went on with the discussion any hopes sank.

'The greys are to be brought up next week from London for I was certain you would want them back. Mr Tattersall has been at me for another chance to market them, but I said that he would have to wait in line for the progeny. He was most interested to know that you would be involved in a breeding programme, my lord, although I did tell him we would not be changing their names.'

'Here's to Maisie and Mick, then.' Daniel raised his glass and laughed. 'But don't give them to me, give them to my wife.'

A strike of excitement flared inside Amethyst.

'Very well, but on the condition that you will

teach my daughter what you know about horses, my lord. She has always been an avid rider, but we have never had the time for more.'

He turned to her. 'Is this something you wish for?'

'It is.' She hoped her father would not notice the expression that she was sure would be in her eyes as she helped herself to a slice of cake.

Indifference was getting harder. The ring glinted against the light, its purple depths lending a richness to the gold and the wine she'd had was making her relax.

Her husband's voice was soft as her father spoke with Julia McBeth on the other side of the table. 'You would like to try your hand with the horses, then? Be warned, though, for the work can be hard.'

He gestured for a servant to refill her glass.

'I have a few mounts of my own in London which I will have brought up. Nowhere near as many as I used to have, but still…'

'Enough to start.'

He smiled and looked at her and the feeling that was hidden in her heart swelled to bursting, though loud footsteps just outside the chamber took their attention.

When a young girl hurried in Daniel stood

and the newcomer threw herself into his arms, her long dark hair loose and her eyes overflowing with tears.

'Andrew Howard…is hurt and…I have…lost Caroline completely.' Her breath was ragged and fast as though she had been running for a long while.

Daniel looked more than taken aback. 'What are you doing here, Gwen? Where is Mama?'

Gwen. His sister? His arms were still about her, though she grabbed his hand now and began to pull him from the room.

'Andrew is outside…I think your man is helping him from the carriage, but Caroline… is at an inn about five miles back.'

'A shabby sort of two-storey building with a large fireplace outside?' When she nodded he asked a further question. 'Why were you there?'

'We were coming to see you as we were worried about you,' the girl wailed. 'Mama forbade us to make the journey to Montcliffe, but Andrew managed to procure a carriage and we came anyway. Caroline needed to stop for…' She left the rest unsaid as she carried on. 'Andrew said he would be our guard…and now he is hurt. Badly I think, because there is a lot of blood and it is all our fault.'

Daniel was already striding outside and everyone followed him. Lucien's younger brother lay on the ground with a blanket over his shoulders, the butler kneeling across him.

'He is in need of a doctor, my lord.' The servant looked worried. His sister simply tipped her head back and wailed, a loud and awful noise that filled all the space around her.

'Stop it.' Daniel gave her no quarter and surprise made her cease. Already he was lifting the boy in his arms and bringing him inside, shouting orders for one of his staff to ride to find the doctor and to another to make ready a bed. Blood dripped across his dress jacket and soaked the bright white fabric of his shirt.

Once the boy was lying on a sofa, Daniel took a blanket from the chair and ripped it into long bandages, fastening them tightly above the injury. The rate of bleeding slowed as he ordered his butler to exert pressure on the offending thigh.

Mrs Orchard had brought through hot water and towels and another pile of quilts, one of which she proceeded to wrap Daniel's crying sister in. Gwendolyn's continued sobbing was obviously getting on everyone's nerves, so Amethyst led the girl to a chair and sat her down.

'When did you last see your sister?'

She could tell Daniel was listening though his attention was still on the injured boy.

'An...hour back. But there...were people there and they were drunk and I could not find her. Andrew was in a fight. The man hit him with a metal pole, I think, and there was so much blood. I knew Montcliffe was close so I helped him into the carriage and brought him here.'

She had begun to shake quite badly, the shock of it all settling in.

'You did well and he already looks better.'

The paleness of Andrew's face was alarming, but he had begun to shiver less violently and accept small sips of sweet hot tea. Daniel moved away.

'Keep them both warm, Mrs Orchard, and give them each some brandy. I am going to find Caroline.'

Amethyst stood. 'I would like to come, too. I am a good rider and you might need a woman to help with your sister.'

Uncertainty flickered across his face, but the situation was too dire to lose any more time in trying to persuade her to stay back.

'Very well. Meet me in the stables in ten minutes. I won't wait longer.'

They rode through the growing dusk at speed, the sound of his horse's hooves matching the beat of hers. He was astonished at her prowess.

If his sister was hurt in any way… He shook away the thought and drew in his reins, waiting as Amethyst Cameron came in beside him. Nay, Amethyst Montcliffe now.

'That is the roof of the inn there.' He tipped his head to listen, music coming from the same direction.

'It's a good sign, I think. If they were hurting your sister, they wouldn't sing.'

He almost smiled, but didn't. Rape followed few rules. My God, he had seen that time and time again in Spain when the whole campaign had fallen to pieces, and the baser nature of men had come to the fore.

'Stay here and mind the horses. If anyone comes, scream as loud as you can and I will hear you.'

'No.' A knife was in her hand, wicked, sharp and ready. 'I can help you.'

'You know how to use it?'

'With proficiency.'

The look in her eyes didn't brook argument. Taking the reins of both horses, he fastened them to a branch. 'Stay behind me, then, and if I say run, you run. Understand?'

Gesturing her assent, she stepped back, the darkness of the riding clothes she had changed into blending with the shadow and reminding him of some of the women in Spain who had marched to the call of the drum and followed their men into battle. Brave and surprising. He liked having her there, a point of reference in the darkness and another pair of watchful eyes.

If anyone had hurt his sister, he would deal with them without a backward glance, he swore that he would. The anger in him shivered over disbelief.

The singing men were outside, gathered around a table and drinking. One was old enough to be his grandfather and the other two looked to be so drunk they would be no threat to anyone save themselves. Motioning to Amethyst, he skirted around a line of trees which brought them up to the front door of the inn. A few patrons were drinking at the bar, but there was no sign of any problem. When a faint noise from above caught his attention, he surged up the stairs and into a room at one end of the passageway.

Caroline was in a corner, crouched down with a broken bottle held out in front of her and her dress ripped down one arm. Three young men were trying to coax her out, their method of doing so bringing a shout from Daniel's throat and filling the room with fury.

A poker sat in one of their hands, the ashes from a fire scattered about their feet. When he looked at his sister again he saw the angry mark of a burn on the bare skin of her upper arm.

The perfect certainty he had always felt in battle suddenly claimed him and he moved forward.

Daniel exploded into action without warning. In less than a minute three men lay at his feet, with barely a noise, hardly a movement. Amethyst had never seen someone fight like that before, the grace of his fury unwinding into a lethal force, the strength of his fists and body simply obliterating any resistance.

Tenderness took over as he brought his sister into his arms, checking her for other injuries and holding her as she shook violently without making a sound.

'You are safe, Caroline. We are here to take you home. Did they hurt you elsewhere?'

'No. They asked me to have a drink with them. I know I should not have said yes, but I couldn't find Gwen or Andrew and so I agreed. They brought me upstairs and I knew then...' She couldn't go on and her brother bent to lift her into his arms.

'Tell me if anyone so much as looks at us, Amethyst.' He made no effort to keep his voice down as he retraced his steps.

Finally they walked out through the front door and into the evening, the soldier in her husband so very clearly seen. No one spoke. No one touched them. No one moved in the stillness of the oncoming night, save them.

Then the horses were before them, whickering at their presence. Amethyst held her knife ready until they were mounted. Daniel threw his cloak around his sister and wrapped her in tight.

'Get on your horse, Amethyst.'

She did it in one quick movement and he tipped his head, gesturing a direction as he spoke.

'They won't follow.' The strength in the Earl's voice was comforting. His hair in the oncoming darkness had fallen loose and lay across his shoulders and he had collected a bruise on his cheek from one flying fist. He had never looked more beautiful to her or more distant.

Much later Daniel called her to his library. Each of the injured young people had been seen to by the doctor and sent to bed and all were expected to have made a good recovery by the morning. Her father had long since retired, but Amethyst had stayed in the downstairs salon reading just to make sure that there was no more trouble.

The Earl was standing at the window as she walked in. He had changed his clothes and now wore a shirt and a loose cravat. His jacket was draped across a chair nearby and he held a drink in his hand.

'Can I offer you something?'

Amethyst shook her head.

'Will you sit for a moment?'

He motioned to two chairs positioned before the fireplace. The grate held the warmth of low embers.

'Caroline was lucky. The doctor said the burn on her arm was superficial and he has dressed and wrapped it. Her fearfulness may take a little longer to recover from, of course, and I doubt she will be venturing anywhere on her own in the foreseeable future. But there is nothing…that she can't recover from.'

'What about Andrew Howard? How is he faring?'

'A little worse. He has a substantial wound on his leg and a large bruise on the back of his head. I have sent word to Lucien who will come to look him over, no doubt.'

'And your mother?'

'Has been informed of the happenings. Unfortunately, I suppose she will also descend upon us.' Drawing a hand through his hair, he continued speaking after a few seconds of silence. 'She is a woman whom life has disappointed and as such goes to great pains to make sure others feel the same way.'

'So she won't like me?'

'Probably not.' He didn't mince the words and for that she was grateful. 'But she does not like me much, either, so we should be about even.'

Shocked, Amethyst looked straight at him. 'But you are her son.'

'She hated my father with a vengeance and I suppose I remind her of him.'

'And Nigel didn't.'

'He was more persuadable and usually did exactly as she wanted. I was less biddable, but families are complicated things and I have long since ceased trying to understand mine.'

Amethyst waited as he took a drink. The bruise on his cheek had swollen and was threatening to close up his right eye.

'Where did you learn to wield a knife?'

Shocked by his directness, she was mute.

'Every other woman of my acquaintance would not know how a blade fits within their fist. But you do. Why?'

She wanted to tell him, she did. She wanted to spit out all the horror of her first marriage in one unbroken line of thought, but this was neither the time nor the place. Not yet. She needed to get to know him better first.

'The docks are dangerous and I was often there at night.'

She didn't know if he believed her or not as he leant forward.

'You surprised me, Amethyst, and that is something not many people have managed to do before. Do you carry your blade now?'

'Yes.'

'Could I see it?'

With only a little hesitation she brought the leather sheath from a deep pocket and laid it on the table between them. To keep a knife on her person in the safety of his home must alert him to some of the things she would rather keep hidden. She also knew that she no longer wished to lie to him.

Picking up the scabbard, he extracted the knife, the multiple grooves on the handle which allowed a better grip taking his attention.

'A double-edged stiletto blade and well balanced, too. Does your father know you carry it?'

She shook her head. 'It would only worry him.'

At that he laughed. 'I am your husband and it worries me. But for now we will leave it at that. I have a request that you might be able to help me with over the next few days. Both of my sisters are…in need of some backbone, for they whine too much and they think too little. Their journey up to Montcliffe today surprised me, however, and made me think there still is a chance to rescue them from my mother's influence, if you like. The thing is, Amethyst, I want them to be more like you.'

'Like me?'

'Stronger. More certain. They have taken on my mother's propensity to complain about nothing and it is wearisome and unattractive. Perhaps with a little coaching and some hours spent in your company they might see the value in pursuing a different path, a braver direction.'

'Should I take this as a compliment, my lord?' Amazement gave Amethyst's words a quiet lilt. 'Most gentlemen of the *ton* want docile wives who think only of the things your sisters are probably fond of.'

'Which is why most marriages in high society are shams.'

Despite everything she laughed. My God, she could never have had this conversation with Gerald, not in a million years.

'And what exactly is our marriage then, my lord, if not a sham?'

The gleam in his pale eyes strengthened. 'You tell me, Lady Montcliffe.' Finishing the last of his drink, he placed it on the table before standing and drawing her up to him, only the smallest of spaces left between them. 'I would also like to thank you for your help today.'

'Thank me?' Every part of her body was squeezed into a breathless waiting.

'It is our wedding night, after all, and even

a marriage of convenience should mark the occasion in some way.'

His fingers stroked the sensitive skin on the back of her neck as he looked at her, the gold threads in his eyes easy to see at such a close distance. 'There are secrets on your face that you might one day tell me and I have my own as well. But right now, here, in this room, there is only the vestige of a difficult evening behind us and the hope of a better day before us. Perhaps we could find it in us to celebrate at least that?'

'How?' She was wary.

'Like this.'

His lips came down across her own with care. He did not force or cajole, he merely waited to see what it was she would do.

A choice, melded with words of thanks and gratitude, a dark night outside and a warmth within. If he had demanded more she might have left, but he did not. The touch of his tongue against her mouth, only asking, and his hand resting lightly against the small of her back.

She did not know what happened between them when they touched, but the same feelings as before rose within her, a longing, an affinity, the woman in her whom Gerald had never discovered pressing forward into the hard edge of his passion, two people melded together in a raw and utter need.

How long had she waited for just this thrall, no rational thought or logic. Her hands went on their own accord to rest on the muscles of his shoulders. Hers. To hold and have. For ever.

But he could not love her back.

The pain of loss rose unexpectedly, spilling into her like ruined wine and making her draw away. She saw need flint in his eyes before distance covered it, the lover swallowed by the soldier as he let her go.

One foot, then two, and although the silence between them screamed with questions she was not brave enough to answer. Yet.

She looked broken and small. He had noticed this thinness from time to time, but tonight it worried him more, her eyes huge in her face, the shadows beneath them dark.

There was something she was not telling him, the shape of it lingering in fear, her breath forcing panic down to a place where she could manage it. If anyone could understand such things, it was him. He tried to set her at ease.

'I like kissing you.'

Her blush was expected, but her tears were

not. He had never seen a woman cry on a compliment before. She wiped them away with the back of her sleeve, hurriedly, as if she had no time for such emotion.

'My father has had the first of the money transferred into your account, Lord Wylde. It should go some way in helping with…' She stopped and breathed out hard, as if she had said too much and did not wish for what would come next.

'With the agreements. Just that?'

She nodded and he felt something shift inside him. Amethyst had been hurt and badly. By Whitely in all likelihood, the husband she had been married to for sixteen months. If she couldn't talk about it, he would ask Robert Cameron privately about the man tomorrow.

A log dropped in the fire and a shower of sparks lit the grate. Home and hearth.

'I want you to know that I would not have married you just for the money.' He dredged up the rest. 'I married you because I liked you.'

This time her smile was real, no pretence in it or anger.

'And perhaps I like you back, Lord Montcliffe.'

'A good start then?'

She nodded and in her eyes was the swell of decision. 'Gerald Whitely was not the man I thought him to be and my mistakes have made me wary.'

He could see what this admission had cost her by the quickened blood pulsing at her throat.

'He came to us as a clerk who was recommended by a friend of my father's. Papa liked him at first, but then he tried to dissuade me from taking the relationship further. I wanted love in a marriage and permanence.'

'But you did not get it?'

'No.' The violent loss in her eyes darkened them, so that they were almost black in the shadows of the room. There could be no mistaking the hatred lurking at the edges, either.

What the hell had Whitely done to her?

'At La Corunna I realised fate could be cheated because I should have died there with a bullet through my thigh and the blood running out of me in a stream, but I didn't. Ever since I have been of the opinion that we each have the choice to worry about what has come before or to forget it.'

A frown marred her brow. 'What of the pain in your leg—does that allow you to forget?'

Her intent told him the question was important and so he took his time in answering.

'Sometimes it does not. In the cold of winter, on the dance floor, after a ride of some distance, at these times I remember. But here with you, in a warm room and on my wedding night, it ceases to demand a constant attention and so the ache itself is lessened.' He stopped for a moment, considering his words. 'You are safe here, Amethyst. I would not ask from you anything you did not wish to give. At least be assured of that.'

Her half-smile wound about the corners of his heart. 'Gerald said that to me, too, and I was foolish enough to believe it.'

And then she was gone, turning for the door and running, the skirt of her riding outfit swishing as she went.

She sat as still as she could and listened. To her heartbeat, to her breathing, to the small sound of her hand as it moved against the silk counterpane.

For so long she had felt…sad. Her father had known of it, but he didn't understand the truth of why. Nobody did. Yet tonight with Daniel Wylde in a room of books and honesty something had changed, some hard part of guilt, leaving room instead for the fluid movement of truth.

She had told him some of it. Just a little, but enough. He could make of it what he would. She knew he had seen the hatred for Gerald in her eyes that could not be hidden, though she wondered about the shame. Had that remained concealed? She hoped so.

Standing, Amethyst walked across to the full-length mirror and simply looked at herself. Against the dark riding clothes her hair caught the light from the candle in a way that surprised her. She almost looked pretty. She had not thought that of herself before, but tonight she did. Perhaps that came from Daniel's kiss. For so long she had been this other woman, frightened by life and lost in her work.

Joyless. Her father had said that about her when he had insisted on this marriage and all its agreements. 'You used to be happier, Amy. You used to know how to laugh. Now you seem only joyless.'

'Gerald.'

She whispered the name into the night. He had taken that part of her that believed in love and possibility and twisted all she had been into who she was now. Daniel had told her the past was gone and could not creep into the present unless you let it. She liked that about him.

'I am enough,' she said, suddenly surprised by how fervently she meant it. 'And my husband enjoys kissing me.'

A power, that, given without the knowledge of what had been taken from her. She held on to his words with hope.

A noise in the room next to hers alerted her to the fact that he had come up to bed and she crossed to the doorway so that she might better hear his movements.

Her eyes went to the key on her side of the portal. If she turned it so that it was unlocked, would he take that as an invitation and come in so that they might talk more? Clasping her fingers tightly together in case she should actually go ahead and do it, Amethyst waited till any noise stilled and then she crept most quietly to her own bed.

The early part of the next morning brought Daniel's sister Gwendolyn into her room, the girl's face uncertain and contrite.

'I hope this is not an intrusion, Lady Montcliffe, but I was wondering if you might have a moment to speak with me?'

Amethyst put down the book she was reading and gestured to a chair beside her. Gwendolyn's dress had been cleaned and pressed, a small tear in the fullness of her skirt artfully repaired.

'I have come to say thank you for your help yesterday in recovering Caroline.'

'You are most welcome.' Amethyst knew there was more to come by the look of intrigue on the younger girl's face.

'Caro said that you wielded a knife. She said that you knew how to use it, too. She told me I was not to tell anyone at all about such a fact and especially not our mother, but…' She stopped and looked uncertain about how to proceed.

'You have questions?'

'Mama is always telling us that we should be docile and sweet and that embroidery and tapestry and reading are the kind of things a husband will be looking for in a marriage. But our brother has been pursued by women for years and years and he did not choose someone like that at all…' The rambling came to a stop as the girl realised what she was saying.

Amethyst picked her words carefully. 'Our marriage might have been a little different from others, Gwendolyn, but I would say to you to be honest to yourself. Be the person you wish to become and follow the interests you want to pursue. Only then will you find a husband who will truly suit you.'

'I love riding and horses and if I could I would live in the country. Mama and Caroline are more interested in gowns and boots and bonnets.' She hesitated before carrying on. 'Are things like fashion and hairstyles important to you, Lady Montcliffe?'

Despite herself Amethyst laughed. 'Not especially. I have only ever had a few gowns at a time and my hair is much too short to do a lot with. From what I can see society seems to dedicate a great amount of time to what one looks like, but I was always too busy helping my father balance books and sourcing timber to care.'

'But you are rich? Richer than anyone else we know?' Gwen's blue eyes flashed fiercely. 'Mama says you come from trade, but it seems to me that you know a lot more than I ever will. You are free to learn things, different things, and in the end you still get to marry an Earl.'

Amethyst did not know whether to tell her of the nature of their union, but then decided against it, choosing to let Daniel's sister see the possibilities before her and not the problems.

'If you would like to come up to Montcliffe Manor to stay with us for a while, you would be most welcome. We could ride together and you could show me the places you liked as a girl when you were here.'

A heavy frown settled across the young brow.

'We did not come here much because Mama never enjoyed it and after Papa died in a riding accident my mother never wanted to stay at Montcliffe Manor.'

'Then we will find new memories, Gwendolyn.'

'Gwen. All my true friends call me Gwen.'

Amethyst smiled. My God, could it be just this easy to fit in? Could the women of the *ton* be exactly like those from the other parts of society; some difficult, some judgemental and others only searching for their way in life? Like Gwen was.

The pathway into the future suddenly did not look so impossible. Amethyst liked Christine Howard and now she understood Daniel's younger sister better, too. How many friends did one truly need?

Reaching over, she took the girl's hand in her own. 'You will find all the things that you need to, Gwen, I promise, and if there is anything that Daniel and I could help you with you have only to ask.'

'Could you teach me how to wield a knife?' The query came back quickly.

'Absolutely.' There were no qualms at all in her answer.

Lucien Howard was at the lunch table when Amethyst came down, as was Daniel, her father and Julia McBeth. Today her husband wore all black, the darkness of his clothes making him look even more dangerous than he normally did.

'I hear felicitations are in order, Lady Montcliffe. Pity I was not invited.' Lucien's voice held a good deal of humour within it.

Daniel's didn't. 'Lucien has come to pick up his brother.'

'I see. How does Andrew fare this morning?'

Lord Ross shrugged. 'He should be down joining us any second. From his recounting of the tale he was the hero of the hour.'

The subject of their musings arrived just as he finished the sentence.

'Who are you saying was the hero of the hour, Luce?' Today a black bruise on Andrew's chin had darkened and he used a crutch to walk.

'You are, Drew.'

Daniel supplied that and his tone sounded grateful. 'If you had not insisted on accompanying my sisters on their foolish journey from London, God knows what else could have happened.'

Charmingly the boy blushed and Amethyst looked away at her father who was in conversation with Julia. The widow brought out the best in Robert and she was glad to see his plate piled high. A new sort of contentment began to fill the empty corners of the past and she caught Daniel's eyes upon her before looking away. The right one had swelled up even further in the night, making him look dissolute.

She wanted to kiss him again, she wanted him to hold her against his warmth and never let go. Her ridiculous heart was beating faster than it normally did just on that one small glance and when she lifted her fork she saw her hand shake.

'You seem flustered this morning, my dear.

Perhaps it is the lingering effects of yesterday's adventure?' Robert remarked.

'Perhaps.' When her father smiled in that particular way her heart sank. She had never been a good liar, that was the trouble. She had never been one of those people who could conceal everything behind an implacable mask.

Like her husband.

'It seems we will be at Montcliffe longer than we had anticipated, but I must say that the area is growing on me. The rolling hills and the greenness and the peace of it all.' Papa was effusive in his praise and Julia laughed.

'Everybody says that after a few days' residence. I could never understand why the Lady Wylde did not come here more often. If it were mine, I should never leave it.'

'But you live here now, do you not?' Papa sounded more than interested.

'Only for another few weeks. I will be travelling north to stay with my sister after that.'

Again Amethyst saw a look on her father's face that made her puzzled, but she could dwell on it no longer as the door opened and a well-dressed woman she had never seen before stood before Daniel, a look of utter disdain upon her beautiful face.

'I have come to take your sisters home, Daniel,' she said, her voice imperious and harsh. 'I also presume that this woman's presence here means that this foolish alliance of yours has already taken place much against my wishes.' Her disdainful glance swept over Amethyst without the slightest degree of interest.

'Indeed it has, Mother,' the Earl replied frostily as he stood. 'This is my wife, Lady Amethyst Montcliffe, and her father, Mr Robert Cameron. I think you know all of the rest.'

'I do.' Lady Montcliffe made no attempt at niceties whatsoever.

'If you would wait in the library, I will come to you directly, Mother, for there are a few things I need to tell you. Gwendolyn and Caroline shall be readied to leave presently.'

But the newcomer was going nowhere. 'Is that you, Andrew Howard? Was it you who put this nonsense into the girls' heads and led them on to a merry goose trail that could have ended in such tragedy?'

The bravado on Andrew's face wilted, though it seemed Lord Montcliffe had had enough of his mother's poor manners as he took her by the arm and shepherded her from the room.

'Daniel's mother was always a difficult woman,' Lucien offered into the silence. 'And his father was little better. Daniel would come and stay with my family most holidays and, looking back, I cannot even remember one where he went home. Nigel came too, sometimes, but he was melancholic and nervous.'

'When he died I didn't feel surprised, really.' Andrew spoke up now. 'Mama used to say that he was not long for this world, remember?'

Lucien took up the tale now. 'Well, Daniel looked after him as best he could, but sometimes even he lost his patience and that's saying something. Nigel was in London when he got home from La Corunna. Daniel had a fever and a leg that looked like it might be septic and he'd lost so much weight from dysentery that the doctors thought he wouldn't make it, yet Nigel only talked incessantly about his own problems. Daniel yelled at him to go away and come back when he was in a better mood, but Nigel was killed in a hunting accident two days later here at Montcliffe.'

'And Daniel blamed himself?'

Her words fell into the silence and Lucien looked at her quizzically.

'I think he did. He seldom spoke of his brother afterwards.'

Glancing around at Julia, Amethyst saw her worried blue eyes were swimming in tears.

Lucien walked into the library late in the afternoon as Daniel was tidying up the deeds from the minister and filing them into the family bible. A marriage of convenience this might be, but it would be recorded in posterity as real. Daniel was glad for that. After yesterday he understood his bride was not the trembling sort of girl that was so predominant in society. No, Amethyst Amelia knew how to wield a knife and ride a horse with the best of them.

Lucien looked more than concerned. 'Could I speak to you, Daniel, in confidence?

The serious tone of his oldest friend alerted him to the fact that something was wrong. 'Of course. Is Andrew—?'

He didn't finish as Lucien broke in. 'After the fracas at the Herringworth ball I took it upon myself to look further into the death of Mr Gerald Whitely and there are things I think you should know.'

Closing the cover of the family bible, Daniel sat down.

'What things?'

'He spent an inordinate amount of time at the Grey Street brothel and word has it that he…he liked to play rough.'

'Damn.'

'My thoughts exactly.'

'Define rough.'

'He gave several of the women there black eyes and split lips. Worse if anyone ever mentioned his…affliction.'

'Affliction?'

'He had had some sort of accident to the groin as a child. I don't know what damage it caused.'

Lord. Had Amethyst ever been hurt by him? he wondered.

Lucien wasn't finished. 'Perhaps Miss Cameron failed to tell you of the relationship between them because it was so terrible. Not lying exactly, just a bending of the truth. She never kept the bastard's surname because…' He tailed off.

'Because he was a bully. Because she was glad he was dead.' Daniel finished the thought for him.

Amethyst with her knife in hand and the ability to use it well. Had she learnt because she had had to? Because she'd had a husband who had taken his anger out on her?

His eyes went to the clock. Too late to try and find out the truth tonight. Yet would she want him to confront her with it tomorrow? His wife was proud, independent and capable and her marriage to Gerald Whitely must be something she would have liked to have forgotten about altogether. He needed her to tell him of it, on her own terms and in her own time.

As a confidant, not an interrogator.

If he picked his moment and had patience she would come to understand that she could trust him.

Finishing his drink, Daniel poured himself another and indicated to Lucien to join him.

Chapter Ten

The next morning began with a fire in one of the cottages and so Daniel was called down to deal with that until well into the afternoon.

When he got back John, the old stablemaster, was waiting for him on the front steps of Montcliffe.

'There has been a mishap, my lord, with Deimos. I took him out into the fields after lunch and he got frisky with a few of the mares. Before I knew it he had taken the fence and gone over into the next paddock, but as he came back one of the younger fillies got in his way and there was a tumble. The long and the short of it, my lord, is that your stallion has a gash on his left fetlock. I knew ye'd want to be dealing with it yourself, so I came up here to find you.'

'How bad is it?'

'Bad enough, I think.'

Daniel's heart sank at the implications. Deimos had been with him in the gruelling Peninsular Campaign and the big black stallion had won over his heart.

Turning for the stables, he was surprised to see his wife waiting for him around the first corner of the building. He was glad that she had dispensed with the brown hairpiece altogether and he wished he might have been able to simply grab her hand and lead her off somewhere to talk. But with Deimos injured his priority lay in the stables. Still, he liked the way she smiled at him, her short golden curls making her look like a beautiful woodland sprite.

'I heard about the accident.'

Her voice was concerned as she stepped into the space beside him. John behind them kept up a low monologue of the way things had transpired all the way to the stables.

'Stay here,' Daniel ordered when they reached Deimos's stall, positioning Amethyst on the other side of the half-door and closing it behind him. Inside Deimos stood, head hanging near the ground and the air of injury about him tangible.

Moving slowly, Daniel went to the steed's

head, allowing the stallion the knowledge of him being there, as he turned his hand against the big muzzle and let him sniffle.

'What's happened?' he crooned. 'I leave you for but a moment and you're hurt. And no war either. Just fillies,' he added, clicking his tongue as the horse raised its head to look straight at him. 'They're always trouble, lad, and it's a fine wonder you have not figured that one out yet.'

Worry sat in the quiet words and the love between them was obvious. By his own admission Amethyst knew that Deimos had carried him through months of chaos in Spain and that they had come home together on the lighters through the winter storms in the Bay of Biscay. What sort of bonds would something like that forge? The tone of his admonishment softened into a whisper as strong fingers slid across a dark topline to the left-hand flank and settled on the leg beneath.

As he knelt, Amethyst balanced on the stall door in order to see better, though when the stallion's tail began to twitch she was suddenly afraid he might kick out.

'Careful.' She tried to keep her voice low,

but the anxiety within had both of them looking up at her in surprise.

'He won't hurt me. He is as steady as a rock, are you not, Deimos, and we have been in far worse scrapes than this one.'

As if the stallion understood he simply turned his head away and stayed still. The stoic lines of the beautiful animal made Amethyst's eyes moisten.

'Is it bad?' When Daniel lifted the injured leg from the ground she held her breath as the blood dripped beneath. If he had sliced open a vein…?

'It's a tear from the knee to the fetlock, but by the looks of it it's missed all the major tendons and arteries,' Daniel answered as he placed the leg down again.

A jagged diagonal wound came into her view, the skin pulled back to reveal the muscle beneath. She noticed he didn't touch it with his fingers, but skirted around the outside as though feeling for something.

'He'll recover,' he said finally. 'With a little luck and some hard work he will be fine again. I'll get the supplies I need now and stay down here with him tonight.'

The light was falling and the dusk burnished

Daniel's hair as he stood. Pulled into a loose queue at his nape, the leather ties were fraying at each end. His beauty never ceased to startle Amethyst. Daniel Wylde's was not a pretty sort of beauty, but a dangerous menacing magnificence that eclipsed all other men. Like the sun in the daytime sky or the full moon hanging low on a summer's eve, one could not remain unaware of his presence. Christine Howard had expressed it well when she had helped her in the preparations for the ball.

'Montcliffe is the man all the girls of the ton *want to take home, but I think he would eat them up before they ever had the chance to tame him.'*

Smiling at such folly Amethyst looked about her. Once the Montcliffe stables must have been magnificent, she mused, for even now in its faded glory the marbled manger and decorative filigree walls caught her attention. Craftsmen had laboured here long and hard on wood and metal and glass. Beneath her feet the floor was inlaid with small stones fitted into patterns that would be easy on horny hooves.

The head groomsman had returned to stand beside her. 'It were a strange accident, my lord, and I am sorry for it. One moment I had his head and the next…'

'I don't hold you at fault, John, but if you could find some empty pails and clean cloths I'd be grateful. I'll get what else I need from the kitchens.'

'Ye'll do the mending yourself then, my lord?'

'I will.'

Daniel had slipped through the door to rejoin her, his mind on the tinctures and ointments he would need, she supposed, a man who would not easily let others do something he could manage himself. Her heart swelled with a kind of aching want; to reassure him, to hold him close against all disappointment, to make this injury disappear and see Deimos well again.

'I would like to help.'

His glance ran across her gown and he smiled, the lines around his eyes deep in the twilight.

'I'll find something else more appropriate to wear,' she added, trying to keep the pleading from her query.

'Very well. It will take me a good half-hour to rustle up the things I need from Mrs Orchard in the kitchen. If you meet me there…'

Walking briskly down the aisle of stones for the doorway, she was glad to go before he had the chance to change his mind.

His wife had not only swapped her clothes, but she had been transformed into a lad, complete with breeches and a shirt. No small metamorphosis either, her legs well defined in the tight pantaloons and the shirt buttons undone around the neck. The most surprising thing was that the outfit looked as though it had been made for her.

'Papa and I travelled in Spain together a few years back. It was easier as father and son at times. I always wore a substantial hat,' she added as his scowl deepened, 'and a coat in public. A long one and well buttoned.'

He wanted to tell her to go and find a jacket now, but the hour was advancing and Deimos needed attention. He hoped John, the old stablemaster, had retired for the night.

Amythest's bottom before him as they traversed the path was round and curvy, little hidden in the cut of cloth or the line of her legs. His wife was tying him in knots and enjoying it for he could see the jaunty lilt in her walk as she turned into the doorway of the stables.

The evening had fallen and although the light was still reasonable he knew he needed more as he followed her in. Striking a lamp, he found an exposed nail and turned it to hold the wire handle. Deimos looked up at him, brown eyes full of liquid hurt.

'Nearly there, lad,' he murmured and lifted the two baskets of supplies into the stall along with a bucket of hot water and cloths. Steam rose in plumes from the pail and the smell of the gathered herbs was pungent.

In Portugal and Spain he had tended to many horses and as his mind centred on what he must do here he bade Amethyst to come in and join him. Another pair of hands would be a god-send and he was glad it was her behind him. Above all the other odours, lemon and laven-der wafted.

'I'll bathe the wound first and then make a poultice. These bowls will be for the chamo-mile and thyme steeped in water for cleaning. If you strip off the leaves, we can make a paste and then add water to it. Warm water, not too hot or too cold.

'All right, Dei?' he asked from his place be-hind the stallion. In response the horse turned, the rope tied to the ring on the stable wall pulling tightly. When he had seen what he needed to he breathed in deep, wrinkled his brow and turned his head away as Daniel began to touch the wound softly, rubbing it downwards. The dirt he could determine embedded in the flesh would come out easily, but from experience it was the tiny particles that you could not see that made a horse sick.

With effort he pushed such a thought away. He would not allow anything to happen to Deimos, he swore it, no matter how long it took to make him better.

A few moments later Amethyst passed him the paste of leaves and he mixed it with water and salt, letting it dribble down the fetlock and seep into the straw. Chamomile stopped inflammation and thyme seemed to hold away the sickness. An old woman in the village here had shown him these remedies as well as others as a youth and he had never forgotten them.

The Montcliffe housekeeper arrived at the stable half an hour later, a pail of boiling water in one hand and numerous rolled bandages in the other.

'If ye'd be needing more, send up word and I'll bring it down.'

'I think this will do, Mrs Orchard. It's just a case of putting in the time and hoping now.'

When her eyes caught sight of what Amethyst had on they widened and she drew back. 'Well, I will be leaving you to it then, my lord.'

'Thank you.'

As she left he smiled. 'It seems she was as shocked as I was by the sight of you.'

'Well, we are married.'

'Indeed. Though in all honesty she probably knows we sleep in separate beds.'

Now it was Amethyst's turn to look horrified and he could not help but laugh as she blushed.

He took pity on her. 'Here, hold this.' The china bowl was exactly what he needed for the poultice and with measures of bran, linseed and beeswax he fashioned a thick paste. Adding a generous dab of fresh honey, he formed a shape in his palm, carefully patting it about the six-inch gash on his horse's leg.

'Give me your hand.'

'Pardon?'

'Your hand. Is it clean?'

She nodded. 'I have had it in the warm water and leaves.'

'Good.'

Depositing the whole concoction in her waiting palm, he guided her to the wound. 'Press like this.' Her skin was warm against his as he crouched down with her between his knees and his mind wandered to a more pleasant imagining. When Deimos whickered, his attention came back and he made himself stand.

'Keep it there while I prepare the wadding. I don't want it to drop off.'

A moment later linen covered the broken skin and she pulled her fingers away in time for the next layer.

Then, placing more salt in the boiling water, Daniel added the rolls of cloth, airing each of them for a few seconds before slapping them on to Deimos's leg and winding them around the fetlock. Amethyst moved to one side to allow him access whilst still holding the bran paste in place, her fingers in spaces he would not have been able to manage had he been alone.

Finally it was finished and, tying the lot off with a series of firm knots, he straightened. The sharp pain in his right leg took a moment to subside.

Amethyst felt Daniel's arm against hers as she stood and so she waited.

For what?

The feel of his body next to her own was familiar and here in the quiet of a windless night she did not want to pull away.

His shirt was wet with the thyme and chamomile tincture, as was hers, the hours of doctoring taking its toll. Realising that both palms were stinging from the heat of the bandages, she opened them to the night air and enjoyed the coolness, fingers splayed.

'Thank you.'

A gratitude that came from his heart. She could hear the tone of it in his voice and see it in his eyes as he watched her.

'I've never seen anyone else manage a wound as skilfully as you did.'

'Then you know nothing of the army. If a soldier can't doctor his own steed, he is in trouble.'

'Even officers?'

He laughed. 'There was not much distinction of ranks towards the end of 1808 as we marched north through Spain through the winter snow. It was each man to his own to simply survive.'

'But you did—survive, I mean.'

'Barely.' Now the laughter was gone.

'I'd heard of it, of course, through the papers and from the tales around London. I even saw some of the soldiers coming off the ships on the south coast. So many men lost and so much blame.'

'You speak of General Moore, I think, but he was a good man who garnered the respect of those about him. Napoleon had upwards of three hundred thousand men at his disposal and we had gone into Lisbon with only thirty-five so to get as many men back to England on the sea transports as the general did was some kind of a miracle.'

Amethyst smiled. Daniel was not a man to blame or whine and moan about things. He just got on with trying his best and fixing it up. Gerald had never stopped in his constant barrage of the wrongdoings of others. She remembered that about him so very clearly it was as if he had only died yesterday.

'I will sleep in the empty stall next to this one tonight just to make certain Deimos does nothing to undo all our good work.'

As the stallion moved Daniel unlatched the half-door and helped Amethyst out, loosening the rope that tethered his horse before joining her.

'Such a night's labour deserves a celebration.' He brought a hip flask from his pocket and undid the cap, offering it to her. When she took it she saw his initials had been placed in the silver, a crest pictured above them.

'It was a present from Lucien a few years back. He bought it in a marketplace in Lisbon and had it engraved there, but the second initial was drawn wrongly.

DCAW.

Daniel George Alexander Wylde.

Remembering his names from the wedding registry, she smiled, though as she took a sip she was not prepared for the strength of the draught.

'Whisky,' he explained, 'and straight from the stills of northern Scotland. It will put hair on anyone's chest.'

Laughing, she handed it back. The top buttons on his shirt had been loosened and the hard lines beneath were easily seen. A man's chest, muscle sculpted and browned. On his right forearm a thick opaque scar trailed from the wrist upwards, disappearing beneath the fabric at his elbow. She wondered how much further it went.

Outside the quiet had settled and the lantern at their feet made the night sky darker. In the ring of flame it was only them, the deep silence punctuated by the snuffling of horses in their various stalls. She made no effort to step back.

As if she had willed it, his finger traced a path from her cheek to her bottom lip. She could taste the salt as she leaned forward, but neither of them spoke as his other hand followed the bones of her neck.

'I want you.'

He was not offering love, but his confession held something more honest because she felt it too, this pull of flesh and bone.

Perhaps lust was exactly what she did need, with chamomile and thyme still in the air and the warmth of healing close. She felt different; on an equal footing in their dirty clothing from the shared task of helping with Deimos, the gap of birth and blood lost amidst more important things.

She wanted more. She did. She wanted the heart, body and soul love her father spoke of and her parents had known. She wanted honesty and strength of purpose.

His lips came across hers slowly, as if to give her the chance to pull back, and in his eyes she saw a question. Then she thought of nothing as his mouth opened upon hers asking for things she had no knowledge of. A force of breath, the feel of his hands, his body pressed tight as he showed her what it was that could exist between a man and a woman.

No small quiet demand either, but in the breaking of a caution she had always kept a hold of, a freedom surged. He would allow her his body without restraint and to do with it as she willed? Nipping at his bottom lip, she felt an answering push, and claimed the response. His gift of acquiescence reflected in the pale green and gold of his eyes.

'You are so very lovely,' he whispered and she felt it, even with her shortened hair and dirty clothes.

'Only with you.' The boldness in her was foreign, unchartered, but when his hand strayed to the buttons on her shirt a new danger surfaced.

Feeling her stiffen, Daniel changed his ploy. He did not want her scared or threatened in any way. Behind them Deimos had moved to the manger and was taking great mouthfuls of the hay stacked in marble. A good sign that, the return of appetite. He smiled into the soft skin at Amethyst's throat and tipped her head to one side so that he might place his mouth across the trembling beat of blood.

'Here,' he said softly as he bore down upon

the spot, suckling in a gentle rhythm, 'and here,' he said again as his mouth moved upwards, the red whorl of his first tasting marked into the white of her skin.

His.

'You are mine,' he said and saw the flutter of her eyelashes, long and silky, the velvet brown of her irises lost in darkness. To have. To hold. To need. No woman ever before had made him feel quite like this. Possessive. Overprotective. Obsessed.

His wife by rule of law and God.

Pushing back the fabric of her shirt, he found soft white lawn and lace beneath, the swell of her womanhood exposed through the open weft. When one finger ran across the proud hard nipple, a cry was wrenched from her throat, pulse racing and breath shallowed.

She did not stop him. Rather she arched into his grasp as though wordlessly asking for what came next. His hand slipped beneath the scalloped edge of lace and cupped one breast. The abundance surprised him, no little bounty here despite her slenderness, and his thumb traced again across a budded nipple.

Dark eyes flew open.

'What is this?' she asked, licking dry lips

with her tongue as she did so, but holding him there, her hand placed across his, the layer of fabric between them.

'Loving, Amethyst, between a man and his wife. No wrongness in it.' His own sex was rock hard and he knew she could feel him, pushing into the space between. Leaning down, he brought his mouth to her breast.

She couldn't think, that was the problem, couldn't place one thought next to another as his mouth did things to her insides she had never thought possible.

This was what she had read about, heard about, wondered of, this connection which did not hold to the bounds of logic. The pull from his suckling speared down into her stomach and lower, every part of her quivering with the touch, balanced on a precipice which she did not want to fall from as she stretched into acceptance.

Nothing else existed here save for them, melded into each other like iron filings in an ancient forge and heated beyond melting point. Shapeless entities save for desire and a knowledge that could not be stopped.

Even without the words of love she wanted

him, her breath fogged in the lamplight and rising upwards.

When she simply surrendered he stilled, her whole being borne to a place that shattered into feeling, waves of release rolling through the tightness, her nails clasped about him like talons in the skin. No time frame or true certainty.

And then a shaking. Of sadness, she was to think later, and of regret. Of missing this for ever and of all the wasted years. Gerald Whitely had made her believe in abstinence and frigidity, her birthmark only sealing in the ugliness, drawn as it was across her top left-hand thigh in a single swathe of red.

His hands moved downwards and into the folds of her breeches. He had lost the struggle to be gentle many minutes ago and his avidity was worrying. In war he was always calm, but here in love a wildness ruled.

The crunch of feet on the gravel a few feet off had him pushing her behind him, though he relaxed as the face of John, the stablemaster, peered through the dark.

'Mrs Orchard sent me down to see if I could escort Lady Montcliffe back up to the house, my lord. She said there is a hot bath waiting and some supper. She'll send food down for you, too, if you are ready.'

He made himself take a deep breath and stepped away from his wife, who was fumbling with the undone buttons on her shirt front. With an effort he tried to find in the interruption some measure of calm as he passed three china bowls across to John.

'If you will take these up with you, Mrs Orchard is wanting them back. Ask her to send down some more water and herbs, if you would, and an apple or two if she has them.'

Amethyst was looking at him, a wobbly uncertain smile on her face, and then she was gone, following the stablemaster up towards the kitchens. Daniel watched her until shadow replaced form and then turned to lean against the wall behind.

He had wanted to take her on the filthy floor of a working stable. The full flush of need left him reeling and he knew he had marked Amethyst with his mouth and that the red whorls of bruising would be even more noticeable on the morrow.

She made him into a man he did not recognise, the more usual temperance replaced instead by a desperate carnal greed. She was his wife, for God's sake, and Gerald Whitely had probably hurt her more times than Daniel could possibly imagine. If he had been allowed the free rein of his desire, could he have done the same? Even now with all these thoughts his rod was stiff and ready, a haze of need making his head buzz and his eyesight blur. A man no better than those soldiers he had seen in the last weeks of the march, any woman young or old a target for their violent ardour.

He had always been in control and had been raised to treat a woman with respect. Until Amethyst. Until the smell and feel of her had burnt into reason and left him crazy.

The ache in his groin intensified and he turned to slam his fist hard into the solid wall behind him, once and then twice more.

Even then the pain did not entirely negate his desperate need and as he swore Deimos lifted his head across the half-wall to watch him.

'We are both of us made damn fools by women,' he said quietly, cradling his bloodied hand as he prayed to God for strength.

Amethyst got up as soon as the first light of dawn crossed the eastern sky and dressed in a sprigged muslin gown with a half-cape to match.

The stables looked deserted as she reached them and, walking down the aisle, she found Daniel tucked into a bed of straw. In sleep he looked younger than he did awake, the lines of responsibility drawn in the daytime upon him lessened in slumber.

'Deimos was restless all night, my lady.'

John had come up to stand beside her, a bunch of fresh straw in his arms.

'His lordship bathed the leg twice more in the early hours and applied fresh poultices. Honey and garlic, I think he used this time, though it's the heat that does it.'

'A difficult night, then?'

'Indeed.' The old man's eyes took in more than she might have wanted, his glance crossing over her colourful gown and carefully brushed hair.

She wished she might stay there and watch over her husband, but she imagined the busy routine of a stables was not one to be easily interrupted and she did not want to be in the way.

'How long will he sleep for?'

'A few hours yet, I'd say, my lady. Deimos reared up at one point when the Earl took him outside and a hoof connected with his bad thigh. Whisky seems to have allowed him some slumber, though it's a two-sided relief. He will have a headache when he comes round and the mood to match it.'

Her eyes took in the top of his right leg where the blanket had fallen away. A smear of old blood had soaked through the fabric of his breeches, darkening the beige into a dirty brown. She also saw his silver flask lying on the straw in a way that pointed to the fact that there was nothing left in the bottle. When she had sipped at it last night the level had been almost to the top.

Unshaved and dishevelled, Daniel looked somehow vulnerable. She wished she could have pulled the blanket up against the chill and covered him, but the stable was quickening into work for the day so she moved back.

'I'll let his lordship know you were here, then, Lady Montcliffe. He'd be pleased no doubt that you came to see how Deimos fared.'

'Thank you.'

'I wouldn't expect him up at the big house for a few more hours yet, mind. That's a fair bit of alcohol he's consumed.'

His laughter followed her outside, though as

she got to the top of the path she saw her father and Mrs McBeth standing together. When she joined them Robert smiled.

'Julia wanted to show me the wildlife in the pond at the front of the house. She also says kingfishers, jackdaws and pipistrelle bats are common around here, so I'm looking forward to seeing those, too.' He frowned as he looked at her more closely. 'You look tired.'

'Lord Montcliffe's stallion was injured and we spent the night in the stables tending to him.'

'All night?'

'No. I returned to the house around one o'clock, but the Earl is still there.'

'Working on Deimos?' The question came quickly from Julia.

'No. He is sleeping.'

When Amethyst caught the light blue eyes she saw worry, understanding and acceptance. Daniel had been her charge for many years, but now she was leaving his well-being to a young wife and trusting her to see him safe. The connection between her and Julia McBeth was unexpected but strong and she saw her father had felt the same sort of affinity for the older woman.

A new beginning for them all then and in a landscape that was both beautiful and peaceful. Even Dunstan House paled against the countryside here and the magnificence of Montcliffe Manor.

Bidding her father and Julia goodbye, she watched them walk together, talking all the way until they were lost from sight.

Today she needed to speak with her husband and be honest about her relationship with Gerald. She needed to tell him things and explain. She also wanted him to kiss her again and hold her in the same way he had yesterday, passion filling every single part of her body.

Snatching at a daisy flower in the grass, she peeled away the petals and chanted an old ditty from her childhood.

He loves me, he loves me not.

The chant continued until a small pile of plucked white was scattered about her.

He loves me...

The last petal. She smiled as she walked towards the house.

Chapter Eleven

The Earl was present for neither lunch nor dinner and when Amethyst asked Mrs Orchard of the whereabouts of her husband, the housekeeper was vague and unhelpful.

Lucien and Andrew Howard had left for London earlier in the day and Gwen had opted to travel with them on the promise that she could return and spend some time with her brother and his new wife the following week. Daniel's mother and her youngest daughter had departed the day before. So it was just her father and Mrs McBeth who were left in the parlour after the night-time meal and both of them looked exhausted.

'Would you mind if we retired early, my love? Julia has planned another morning ramble for me to enjoy tomorrow and I don't want to miss it.'

Amethyst was amazed. Her pale, thin and ill father seemed here to have been given another lease on life. Even his clothes seemed to sit on him better.

'Of course not, Papa. I was about to go up myself.' Her eyes glanced at the ornate timepiece on the mantel. Eight o'clock. Perhaps she could find a book in the Montcliffe library before she went upstairs. The thought cheered her.

A few minutes later she stood in front of the bookcase and perused the contents. All manner of tomes graced the shelves, from the weighty pens of the ancient Greek philosophers to the lighter one of Maria Edgeworth's *Tales of Fashionable Life.* She smiled. She could not in a million years imagine Daniel Wylde reading that.

Where was he? she thought. Was he in his chamber or had he been called away? She had caught sight of John earlier and asked after Deimos. By his account the stallion was on the road to recovery and the Earl had left the stables after the midday lunch.

Back in her room, she crossed to their shared doorway and stood to listen. No noise or movement could be heard on the other side, which led her to the conclusion that he was not there. Another thought surfaced. Had he regretted their marriage already and journeyed back to London? Perhaps Andrew had worsened or Caroline? She could not believe the Earl wouldn't at least have informed her of something so terrible and pushed the notion away. She wished it was last night again and that they were in the stall with his stallion. She wanted to feel his mouth on her breast and find the love marks on her body as she had this morning when she had taken off her nightgown.

Surprising. Drawn in passion. Treasured. All the feelings that Gerald had never been able to give her with his accusations and his anger. Her fault, he had said, but increasingly she was beginning to understand that the problem had been his own and that in her innocence she had not comprehended such a falsehood.

In the stall last night Daniel's manhood had pressed against her in a way she had never felt Gerald's do. Oh, he had kissed her nicely at first and at least with some modicum of need, but she had not seen any outward sign of masculine lust.

With Daniel it was entirely different and it was addictive to think that she, the plain and boring Miss Amethyst Cameron of her first husband's angry tirades, might affect the one man whom every lady, young and old, of the *ton* coveted.

Lord Montcliffe liked her. He liked kissing her and he liked her blushes and if John the stablemaster had not interrupted them she was sure her husband would have asked for…more.

She fanned her face with her hand and crossed the room to look at herself in the mirror. The whorls of red still showed in the crease of her neck and across the swell of her bosom. Thrilling reminders as she flicked her thumb across her nipple in the same motion as he had and a sharp pain of want pierced thinly. Changing. Quickening. For so long she had been afraid of everything and now she wasn't.

Tears sprang to her eyes, the hope in her reflection obvious. Would Daniel want her as much as she wanted him? Would he allow her to make the first move or was it proper to wait for a man to initiate intimacy?

Another worry then surfaced. Would the birthmark on the top of her left thigh be as much of a problem for him as it had been for Gerald? He had hated the mark and on the few occasions when they were first married and he had tried to take her to his bed he had been unable to remain there. She had not known much of what should have happened between a man and a woman, but she knew enough to understand his deep loathing of her own inadequacies.

'You are ugly,' he had railed, 'and you make no attempt at all to entice me. Ugly, thin and marked.'

The embarrassment of such words still lingered, anger and shame there in the mix, but also puzzlement. She could not imagine Daniel shelving his masculine passion for such a thing.

The small fire in the grate sparked and a handful of red embers glowed against the back of the chimney. If they stayed there whilst she counted to five everything would be all right, but if they faded…

Closing her eyes, she chanted the numbers quickly, pleased to see the sparks still lived against the dark and sooty framework when she opened them again.

The signs were changing, she thought, and for the better. The petals the other day and now the sparks. Perhaps things would be all right, after all, and the hopes and dreams she had of this marriage would come to pass. Threading her hands together, she knelt beside her bed and prayed her very hardest that the sort of love her parents had enjoyed might be transferred to their lives as well.

Breakfast the next day was a strained affair. Amethyst had been married for nearly four days and yet she had seen her husband for less than twelve hours during all that time.

Her father ate quietly next to her as she picked at the scrambled eggs she had on her plate. Julia on the other side of Robert looked worried as well.

'I was certain Mrs Orchard would know something of the movements of the Earl, though she swore that she did not when I asked her this morning.'

'Is it normal for Montcliffe to simply just disappear like this?' Her father asked that question.

The older lady shook her head. 'No, I imagine it is most unusual unless he has been called away to London, which could be the case.'

'He said nothing to you at all, my love?

'We were busy with the stallion, Papa. The next morning I went down to see how the Earl had fared, but he was asleep. The horse had been restless by all accounts in the night and the old stablemaster told me that Lord Montcliffe had tended to it.'

'How is Deimos now?' Julia's question held concern.

'I'll go down to see John after breakfast and ask. I had not imagined Lord Montcliffe to just leave Montcliffe Manor given the stallion's accident and that is what is so strange.'

She did not add that from her point of view his disappearance was also surprising. Their last meeting had been full of the promise of more intimacy and to find herself left without an explanation was odd.

'Julia and I are off to look at various houses in the area today. Perhaps you would like to come and join us? We could pack a picnic and have it by the river for the weather is mild and no rain is predicted.'

Amethyst shook her head. A whole day away from Montcliffe Manor and the hope of seeing Daniel was not a prospect she looked forward to.

'Thank you for asking me, Papa, but I think I will visit Deimos this morning and take him some fruit.'

An hour later she hung on the half-door and watched the enormous stallion. Today he was ready to greet her and far more interested in his surroundings. The left fetlock still held a bandage, but he did not favour the leg as he once had.

'Hello, beautiful.' She held out an apple brought from the kitchen and the horse took it from her, crunching down the fruit in seconds. 'I see you are a lot better. Your master will be most pleased.'

'Oh, indeed he is,' John said from behind her. 'He asks morning and night about Deimos's progress.'

Amethyst's heart began to beat faster. Morning and night? He was here somewhere, then? Her eyes took in all the corners of the stables and saw nothing.

'You have been speaking to my husband?'

The old man frowned. 'Of course.'

'Where is he?'

'In the annexe, Lady Montcliffe. It's Mrs Orchard's hope that the fever will be breaking soon, though from what I can see…'

Fever? The annexe? What on earth had happened?

'Where exactly is the annexe, John?' Amethyst tried to keep her voice even, but the pitch had risen considerably and for the first time in their conversation the old stablemaster looked uncomfortable.

''Tis behind the main house, my lady, through the kitchen gardens and out the back. It used to be the quarters of the Earl's grandfather, so it is well furnished and comfortable. If you get lost, ask any of the servants and they will give you direction.'

'Thank you.' She walked away at a pace that she hoped would not draw attention, but every part of her wanted to break into a run. Daniel was here and he was sick and she had not been told anything of it at all. The anger in her mounted as she strode around the corner to the kitchen.

A serving maid walked down the path with a tray of untouched food as she approached the door, her face paling as their glances met.

'My lady…I think Mrs Orchard would like to see you before…'

'Oh, I am more than certain that she would,' Amethyst returned, her tone cutting. Continuing on, she gave the girl no more attention and was glad the servant seemed to have decided reinforcements were needed, her retreating footsteps becoming fainter and fainter.

The room was dark when she opened the

door, and hot, a good ten degrees warmer than the summer's morning outside and it took a moment for her eyes to acclimatise from sun to shadow. Then she took in breath. Nothing made any sense here, the dying stalks of reeds in vases and the ancient carcase of an animal on the table strung out with pins and beads. The air around her was filled with the smell of pitch and sulphur.

A crunch beneath her feet made her look down. Eggshells, crumbled into pieces and mixed with what looked to be apple and bread. On the table in the middle of the room old bottles were arranged in a long line with bags of canvas above, the brown sediment dripping from each corner collected in a large brass pail. A jar of honey and several dishes of dried spices sat next to them with pills in brown paper twists, all opened to show a good many had already been administered.

A groan of pain took her attention.

'Daniel?'

The noise stopped.

She was in the smaller rear chamber in a second and there in a bed of blankets her husband lay, woollen fabric wrapped around his head and his face crimson with the heat. When he saw her recognition flinted and his hand came up.

'Go...away...'

But she had already seen what he was trying to hide. His naked right leg was swollen to three times its normal size and the flesh of his thigh was purple and mottled.

'My God.' She was across the room in a second, the flat of her palm against his skin on his forehead. Heat radiated out, the dryness of it more worrying than anything else. Pale eyes watched her, grimacing as he failed to sit up.

'Stay still,' she ordered and began to strip away the heavy bedding before crossing to the windows and opening them. The air came rushing in, a draught that dispensed somewhat with the awful smell of sulphur and pitch and rustled the lawn curtains. Returning to his side, she snatched the wool from his head and threw the thing right out of the window. It sailed past the astonished presence of Mrs Orchard.

'What do you think you are doing?' The housekeeper's voice was furious. 'His lordship has expressly told me that you were not to know of this, ma'am. He wants to handle it in his own way, he does, and if he could talk I am certain he would be asking you to leave.'

'Get...out...now.' Amethyst did not even try to moderate her anger. 'And send John the old stablemaster in to me immediately.'

The woman looked as though she might argue, her face crimson with anger, but thinking better of it she turned on her heels and left. Daniel simply allowed his head to fall back against the pillows, all energy spent.

Her palms touched his thigh and he let out a cry. 'It serves you right that this hurts so much.' She pressed harder, determining the flesh was swollen but not putrid. 'You spent all of one night and the next day tending to your horse and yet you did not think to help yourself. The village doctor will be sent for immediately.'

His right hand snaked out and caught her arm. 'No…not…doctor.' His voice was rough and his lips were dry. A small smear of honey would fix that, but it was the entreaty in his eyes that made her hesitate.

'Why would you not call a doctor?'

'My…physician…wants…it off.'

Then she remembered. He had told her of this fear once before and it explained everything. The strange and quackish medicine of Mrs Orchard, the hidden annexe and the secrecy. My God, he truly believed he would lose his leg and this was his method to try to save it?

She removed the blanket and looked down. Mrs Orchard had cut the trousers away almost to the groin and the flesh pushed hard against fabric.

A series of bottles next to his bed also caught her notice. *Emetic. Purgative. Clyster.* The labels were carefully drawn in a hand that was precise and bold. Gathering all three together, she walked to the window and calmly hurled them after the strange woollen hat. There was a smashing of glass and then silence.

His pale eyes contained just a hint of humour as she rejoined him. 'Now that we have got rid of those we can start to get you better. Certainly you will never recover if this quackery is all you receive.'

His lips turned up slightly, heartening her. Surely there could be no humour left in someone who was dying?

'And while we are at it I'd like to say that being married means just that. Someone by your side. Someone who will fight for you. Someone that cannot be pushed away when things get difficult. I should expect that from you if I were sick and so whether you like it or not you are going to get just the same from me.'

A slight cough behind her made her turn.

'Ahhh, John. I am glad that you are here because I wish for you to fetch chamomile and thyme, honey, bran, linseed, hot water and bandages. And beeswax, wasn't it? All the things we used on Deimos's fetlock. And a good wad of linen.'

His smile told her that he would comply. 'Oh, and tell Mrs Orchard to leave the pails of boiling water at the door when she brings them, for I do not wish to see her.'

Through the haze of pain Daniel realised Amethyst was ordering everyone around and that the fit of temper made her eyes more golden and her cheeks a flushed pink.

Damn it, why did she not leave him to his fever and his suffering? He did not want to be poked and probed and made ready to have his leg severed. He just wanted to die here, whole and complete, the life in him flowing out by degrees.

He didn't want her to see his leg either, the ugly hugeness of it or the scars. He wanted to turn away on the bed and have her gone, disappeared, only the purgatives left, and the medicines that made him so sick he forgot everything else.

His brother had cheated this sort of death with a quick bullet to his temple, but he had not been brave enough to do the same. If his leg went, Amethyst would be saddled with a cripple for the rest of her days and the things they had planned to do together like riding would be lost. He didn't even want to contemplate what an amputation might do to any prowess in the matrimonial bed. He would be bloody useless and because she was kind she would pretend he wasn't. God, help me he thought, as his wife's small hand came into his own and his fingers closed about them.

Holding on.

The tears on his cheeks surprised him, but he could not even turn his head away.

She felt his plea and knew his pain, but she made herself staunch. A wife who went to pieces was not what he needed now at all and she was damn well going to chase him to the afterlife and back to make certain that he did not die.

'I love you.'

There, she had said it out loud into the room, with all its clutter and its debris and the tears on her husband's face. 'I have loved you since the first moment I saw you on the steps of Tattersall's because you are strong and beautiful and good. If you die, I will too, I swear it, from a broken heart and a broken life. So if you have any decency at all you will fight to survive this and you will fight hard.' His glassy eyes watched her, the fever marking spots of red into the white, and barely blinking. 'I will love you for ever, damn you, Daniel Wylde. Do you hear that? It's for ever with me.'

She could not make it plainer, but already he looked to be slipping into sleep. If she shook him awake again, would it be better or worse for him? With no other experience in healing save that with the stallion she simply stood and watched, making certain his chest rose and fell, and was pleased when the old stablemaster came back with the supplies they needed.

'The village doctor has been sent for, ma'am, but Mrs Orchard asked me to tell you that Dr Phillips is at least two hours away at a difficult birthing for the maid in the parlour has a sister who works for him.'

'Then we will start without him. The fever

needs to be brought down and the wound to his leg has to be dressed. I had thought to treat it in the same way the Earl treated Deimos.'

Unexpectedly the older man smiled. ''Tis not much difference between the wounds of a man or a horse, to my way of thinking, ma'am, and if Mrs Orchard's home remedies have brought the master to this bad pass then I'd say it's time to try something else.'

'You think it will work?'

'It did a treat with the stallion, though it took a few days. The wound has the same sort of look to it and there is no worse damage to the flesh that I can see.'

'You'll help me then?'

In reply he rolled up his shirtsleeves and set to stripping the leaves of chamomile and thyme into the warm water before adding a lump of salt to the brew.

Amethyst cut away the last of the breeches with her knife, pleased for the long shirt the Earl wore to cover his modesty. Still, her cheeks flared with the endeavour and she hoped when a nightgown had been sent down from the house and they dressed him later, he would not ask who had cut away the last of his trousers.

The chamomile-and-salt paste obviously

stung him even in his unconscious state, for he rolled from side to side trying to get away from their ministrations. It took her a long time to brush the wound out with the linen until it looked a healthier pink.

As John readied the poultice she saw he had added his own mix of ingredients, which differed a little from those Daniel had applied to Deimos. Comfrey, angelica and feverfew were just a few of the herbs she recognised, but he had also peeled many cloves of garlic and crushed them into the paste. When he applied it to the wound the balm seemed to hold its shape with ease and she asked him about it.

'It's the stickiness of comfrey that does it, my lady. My mam used it all her life on us and I never forgot. Once Da lost three toes in an accident with an axel and she had him walking in weeks. Didn't turn bad, neither.'

The linen wadding and hot bandages came next and when the last of it was applied John positioned the Earl's wounded leg on a high stack of cushions.

'Can't do this with the horses, ma'am, but I would if I could. It does wonders for the drainage.' He stood back. 'Now with a good amount of thin chicken broth in him and the windows open he has the chance to get well.'

Amethyst reached for his hand, both their palms reddened from the heat and dried with white lines from the salt. 'I will never forget this, John.'

He smiled. 'You've the way with his lordship that he needs, I think, ma'am. It's been a rough few years with the army and his brother so a bit of peaceful rest will do him good. I will tell Mrs Orchard to send one of the maids over with that broth. Make sure you have some, too.'

When he left Amethyst used the time to clean up all the basins and pails and twigs that were left around the floor. The village doctor had finally arrived, but on seeing what she had done had informed her that he could not have managed better and then left. The birthing he had been attending was a difficult one and he needed to get back, though he promised to return to Montcliffe in the morning.

Drawing out a thin clean sheet from a large linen cupboard Amethyst arranged it across her husband, tucking in the top around his chin. Later she would find lavender for the room and perhaps a scented candle, but for now a tiredness descended upon her. Pulling a chair up to the bed, she dropped into it, glad to be off her feet.

* * *

It was dark and late and the pain that bloomed at the edges of his mind pulled him awake so quickly he felt the thumping of his heart in his chest.

Daniel's glance fell downwards and he saw his leg propped up with pillows and bandaged from groin to knee. As he wriggled his toes the relief that swamped him was enormous. It hadn't gone, then, and he still retained the feeling.

The days of being sick ran into each other, though he remembered Amethyst shouting something at him, anger in her eyes. He remembered John here, shadowed through the heat of a steamy room. He thought Dr MacKenzie from London had been by the bed at some point too, prodding at him and opening his eyes. But now there was only a dark silence.

He was alive and the breath he took no longer hurt in each and every part of his body. The room was clean, with cool, fresh linen arranged across him and the awful smell of sulphur gone.

He tried to lift his arm to wipe his dry lips, but the energy needed defeated him. Instead he turned his head and saw his wife on the leather chair and fast asleep. In stillness he watched, her small breaths rhythmic and deep, and the silky lashes on her cheeks long in repose.

Parts of the past days came back through the ether. The heat of the bandages, the smell of garlic, a cold flannel gently wiped across his forehead, water dribbled between dry lips.

I love you.

He stiffened, trying to catch the cadence of the words.

Had she said it or had he?

Tiredness swamped him and even the light of a candle burning on the mantel seemed too bright. He groaned.

'You are awake?' Her voice was soft as she came from slumber, but he could only watch her, the wheat-and-gold curls held back with a band of dark blue cloth.

'You have been ill. John and I have been tending to you and the fever broke this afternoon.'

Leaning over, she applied honey to his lips. He could not even lick away the sweetness. 'I will find you a drink for I am sure you must be thirsty.'

Standing, she went from his sight, but her footsteps were close. Then she was back, one hand cradling his head and bringing him up. The fresh water was sweet and cold, though she allowed him only little sips.

'Too much will make you vomit again.'

Again.

'Your physician was called from London and he said to give you only tiny amounts until your stomach can manage it. He says it will be a few days until the sickness subsides.'

'MacKenzie was here, then?' Nausea rolled through his body in slow and undulating waves.

'Is here. Mrs Orchard has put him up in the house. He is pleased with your progress, too, because the swelling on your leg has gone down and the colour is better. There was a blockage and he removed it.'

A blockage? The bullet?

Daniel tried to ask her about it, but he could not. The skin beneath his wife's eyes was bruised purple and the scratch from the ring on her cheek had scabbed. Exhausted. Because of him. Where was Mrs Orchard? Why were the servants not here helping her?

Swallowing, he spoke, though the words came out as a whisper.

'Thank…you.'

Tears welled in her eyes before she wiped

them away with a quick and embarrassed dash. He saw that her hands were blistered and with a huge effort reached out for the one that was nearest.

'Sorry.'

He was asleep again before she could even answer, his fingers limp and warm. Sorry I have been sick? Sorry I cannot love you?

Had he heard? Would he guess? Did he remember what she had told him in the quiet watches of his illness? And now that he was getting better, how did she hide what she truly felt?

She couldn't and the danger of it all spiralled.

Bringing his fingers to her lips, she kissed each one, strong fingers with war imbued within them, no pampered and indolent lord, but a man who had lived through battle as well as peace and who had defended himself and his country.

A knock on the door took her attention and, laying his hand down on the counterpane of the bed, she crossed to see who was there.

Her father stood on the top step, question on his face. 'I wondered if you were coming back up to the house this evening. It is late?'

She shook her head. 'I think I will remain here tonight, Papa. Lord Montcliffe is restless and may need me.'

'Every man needs his wife, my jewel, especially one who has been so sick.'

'I love him, Papa.'

'I know.'

'I am not certain if he loves me back.'

A small frown crossed his face and then a smile. 'Your mother would have said listen for things other than the words, Amy, and she would have told you to be patient. Love comes in many forms,' he added and reached forward to lift up the gold cross at her neck. 'It is here in your mother's gift and there in your blistered hands. Look for it in Daniel Wylde, Amethyst, but do not be greedy. Men can sometimes be afraid of love.'

'Were you?'

'When I first met your mother I was. And now…' He stopped himself before saying more, but she saw secrets in his eyes.

'It is Julia?' Her question held no regrets.

Without hesitation he nodded.

'I have seen a house not far from here for sale. It has a garden that runs from the steps at the front to a lake beyond it.'

As he spoke he beamed in a way she had not seen him do for so very long.

'If you are to live at Montcliffe Manor I would like to be close. Julia has expressed an interest in living around Barnet as well for she has no fixed abode to call her own. I know my heart is weak and there may not be many months left for me, but still…?'

And then Amethyst knew. The truth as it must have been for all the days of their visit. Her father was enamoured with Julia McBeth, with her light brown and curling hair and her gentle pale blue eyes. A kind woman, a good woman. A woman who might see him comfortable and looked after for these last months or hopefully even years of his life.

'Susannah said to make you flourish, Amethyst, and I think you will here, but I also need a life. Do you approve?'

She flung herself into her father's arms and showed him with every ounce of love just how delighted she was with his choice of both companion and of abode.

'You know that I do. Anything to make you happy and relaxed were what the doctor ordered and this seems exactly that.'

When he had gone Amethyst sat again at

Daniel's side. She felt safe finally. Indeed, if she had her way she would stay well out of the way of society and cocooned in the green heart of the countryside for ever.

Chapter Twelve

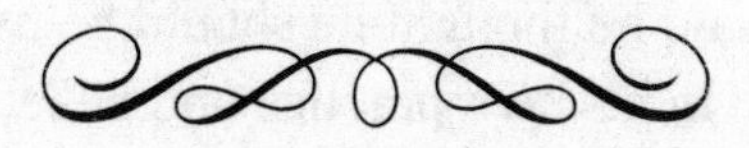

She was there watching him when he awoke again.

'I cannot be...good company.' The words were easier to say now. 'If you wish to go...'

'I don't.'

'It is late?'

She nodded and he looked across at the window. The curtains were not drawn and the light of a full moon fell into the room. After one o'clock, at least, and more like nearly two from the slant of shadow.

'Dr MacKenzie has had to go back to London, but he insists that you are being left in able hands.'

'Yours?' He smiled and moved his foot, bending his knee so that he could see the bandage and reassure himself that his leg was still there. Pain shot into his thigh, but it was bearable now, a lesser hurt. 'It looks a lot like Deimos's fetlock.'

'John helped me.'

The lines from his eyes crinkled with humour. 'What did MacKenzie say?'

'He said he thought he should be using the poultice in his own practice and he left something for you. He was certain you would be pleased.'

Leaning over to the small cupboard beside the bed, she took out a dish and picked up a bud of hard metal.

'This bullet came from your thigh.'

Relief rushed through him, making the blood beat in his ears. 'He got it out, then?'

'Dr MacKenzie said that the swelling dislodged it from the bone. He has never seen that happen before. He also said that I was to get you up walking as soon as I could.'

Daniel couldn't believe the elation of knowing he hadn't died or been left badly crippled by an amputation. He wanted suddenly to go outside into the light of the moon and feel the cold air upon his face, to put weight upon the bone and feel it strong and usable and real.

Shimmying up on the pillows, he moved his

legs around to the side of the bed. His thigh throbbed, but he made himself wait until his body became accustomed again to the new position.

'I hope it was not you who had to dress me?' His nightshirt was long and bulky. There was nothing underneath it save his skin.

When she coloured he muttered something softly under his breath.

'John fashioned this for you.' Amethyst handed him a stick carved from hard wood. Its handle had been made into the head of a stallion, the rippled seams of dark knots giving the illusion of a mane. The cane felt good in his hand and sturdy as he stood, imbalance keeping him still until the world righted again.

Limping outside, Daniel sat by the front door on a chair Amethyst had placed there, the herbs from the kitchen garden pungent. He was relieved to be away from the bed.

'Nigel and I used to play here when we were young. Julia would bring us treats from the kitchen.'

'She is a good woman.'

He nodded.

'My father is most enamoured of her.'

Daniel smiled and for a moment they stayed

quiet, nothing between them but silence, though his mind raced with all the other questions he needed answers for now that he felt stronger.

'Did Whitely ever hurt you, Amethyst?'

Even at a distance he could tell that she stiffened. 'Why do you ask?'

'Lucien said the man had a reputation for striking out with his fists in the heady dens of London's most expensive brothels.'

She breathed out hard before answering. 'He had a sickness, I think, that he could not control.'

'Did he hurt you?' The anger in his voice was obvious, but even with effort he failed to soften it.

'He was a man prone to high emotion that he had no way of controlling, you understand, and on top of that he liked to drink. More and more as our marriage progressed and he realised that our union had been a terrible mistake. It was probably my fault, too, because by that time I knew I could not abide him anywhere near me and I said so. The night-times were the worst because he was not able to...' She stopped and took a deep breath, reasoning Daniel would hardly wish to hear about their more intimate problems. 'He lashed out with words at first and then with his fists. A month after our nuptials he lost control and punched me in the stomach, as hard as he could. He told me that he could ruin my father's reputation completely with some of the things he knew and I believed him.'

'What happened next?'

'I was sick all over his boots.'

'God.'

'So he left and did not come back again for nearly a fortnight afterwards. By then I had arranged a tutor in the art of self-defence, using the same knife that you saw me with the other day. He never touched me again.'

'Never?'

'He had discovered other women who were more than pleased to accommodate him. He had our money behind him and was in the process of setting up his own dubious business schemes, which we knew nothing of until it was too late. Besides, I was more in the way than anything and he made certain to tell me I was ugly every time he saw me.' She took a deep breath and went on. 'I have a birthmark on the top of my left thigh, the kiss of the fairies my mother used to tell me it was, but to Gerald it was the stamp of the devil.'

'And to you…what is it to you?'

She turned away, but not before he had seen her tears. 'It was my shame.'

The shame of her own feebleness and paralysis. The shame of allowing another governance over sense and strength. The shame of not telling her father all that was happening and yet failing to deal with it well by herself.

She could tell Daniel wanted to say something by the anger that flicked across his brow, but he didn't. Rather he took her hand in his and they sat there, just the two of them, her perched on the top step and him on the dainty inside chair, watching the sky and the stars and the large full moon above them.

Finally he spoke. 'Marks on the body show the journey of life, Amethyst. Were we to survive every year unblemished I doubt we would have truly lived.'

He lifted the sleeve of his nightgown and she saw the same wound she had once before noticed, this time uncovered. 'It is not pretty, I know, but if I touch this I think of how lucky I was to survive.'

'What happened?'

'My brother pushed me into a grain machine when I was nine.' He smiled then, his white teeth easy to see in the moonlight. 'Nigel got the fright of his life, but the scar turned out to be a godsend. Every time he played roughly after that I made sure he got a glimpse of it and he usually stopped.'

His thumb stroked her wrist and he looked across at her. 'This is the same sort of badge. You prefer carriages moving at the slowest of paces and who can blame you for that? Look at Whitely as another lesson, but know that one foolish marriage doesn't mean you have made another.'

She couldn't help but frown at his logic. 'But I did not decide to marry you for any other reason than to make my father happy in the last months of his life. A reason that was foolish to the extreme in any way you might look at it.'

'Then it's lucky I am nothing like your first husband…' he returned and laughed out loud, the sound ringing in the empty chambers of her heart and filling them with gladness.

My goodness, how she loved him. She wanted to say it out here with the night-time masking her shyness, but she couldn't. He was still weak from all he had been through and he needed to be back in bed. Besides, if he did not feel what she did everything would change and she could not risk such disappointment. Better to leave it as it was, the hope of something, the taste of possibility. When he recovered there would be plenty of time to talk.

He awoke to her there in the morning curled upon the bed beside him and for the first time in days his body seemed free of heat and sickness. She lay in a full day gown on top of the counterpane, a pillow carefully positioned between them. Her hair was loose from the band she wore and the curls jostled wildly in short lengths of gold and blonde.

Beautiful. More beautiful than any other woman he had ever known, inside and out.

The revelation was startling. He had not married an *ingénue* who would take fright at things out of the ordinary. He had not married a society princess either, with a constant want for the very best and the most expensive. Amethyst Amelia was brave and true and real, a woman who would walk by his side and watch over him as he would her. A partner. A friend. A lover, too, if he could ever get his strength back.

Gerald Whitely by her own admission had been a brute of a husband. The stakes had heightened. He needed to woo his unusual bride and court her and make her understand that without him life was…unliveable. He smiled at such melodrama, but inside he knew he had finally met the woman who completed him and so very unexpectedly.

Firstly, however, he needed to get better.

'You are certain you do not need my help?' She finished fussing with the things on his bedside table just to make sure that he had all he needed and close by.

He had moved back into his room at Montcliffe this morning and much to his surprise Robert Cameron had hired a good many extra hands from London to make certain that he was well cared for.

'No, all is in order, Amethyst,' he said from his place in the wingchair by the fire. He had dressed this morning in his own clothes and his hair had been trimmed.

'You can do something for me before you go, however. Could you send your father to see me?'

'Now?'

'If it is possible.'

'Of course.'

Daniel saw the puzzlement and question in

her eyes, though she said nothing as she gave him her goodnight and let herself out of his chamber.

The formality between them since leaving the annexe broke his heart, but there were things he needed to do first to make this marriage right. For her sake and for his.

Robert arrived a few moments later. He looked far healthier than he had in London, and happier. The influence of Julia McBeth, Daniel supposed, and gestured for his father-in-law to take a seat near him by the fire.

'Thank you for coming so quickly.'

'Amethyst said it was important.'

'It is, although I did not enlighten her as to what it was I needed to say to you.'

'I see.' A heavy frown covered the brow of the other and he fidgeted with a handkerchief he took from his pocket.

'Can I offer you a drink?

'No, thank you, my lord. The hour is late and I would not sleep well if—' He stopped abruptly. 'I am an old man now, Lord Montcliffe, and age leads me to say things that I could not have as a youngster.' He took breath. 'My daughter is a good honest woman and if you think she is not quite the wife you want I would urge you to give it more time because—'

He didn't finish because Daniel interrupted him.

'I want to ask for Amethyst's hand in marriage, Mr Cameron, but properly this time.'

Astonishment made the other's eyes wider. 'But you are already married, my lord.'

'I need the conditions and amendments gone. No limits anywhere. A true marriage.'

Robert suddenly seemed to get the gist of what he was asking, for his cheeks reddened with emotion. 'You want for ever?'

'I do.'

He cleared his throat. 'Then I would be most honoured to revoke any conditions and give you my wholehearted blessing.' With intent, he thrust out his hand and the Earl took it. A handshake to nullify convenience. 'I have dreamed of this, of course, and hoped it might come to pass, for Amy has been happier here than I have ever seen her.'

'Then that brings me to another matter altogether.' Daniel's voice was measured. 'That of Gerald Whitely.'

Robert paled at the name.

'I am surprised that as a doting father you

did not realise the man's true nature and deal with him.'

'True nature?'

'On Amethyst's own admission he hurt her physically. Then he proceeded to break down any belief in herself.'

'I know.'

'Pardon?' The anger in the word was harsh.

'I made it my business to find out all that I could about Whitely after Amy married him, Lord Montcliffe. A friend of mine had sent him to me with a high recommendation, but as a father I could see how unhappy he was making her. The discoveries I made were not comforting. Each fact I found out seemed worse than the last one, for he had confounded us into believing he was something he most definitely wasn't.'

'Which was a fraudster with violent tendencies?'

'I see you, too, have done your homework. But he was all that and worse. It was he who tried to murder us in the carriage accident on the way to Leicester. If we were both to die, all the Cameron money would be in his hands and since niceties between us had long since broken down I could not trust that he wouldn't try it again when we survived. I had him followed one night in London by a chap called Black John Lionel who was known in the docklands as a fixer, a man who might scare others off their chosen course of action, you understand.

'He found Whitely alone in a brothel he frequented in Grey Street with two shots through the head. A youngish gentleman had pushed past him in a hurry to leave as he had walked up the stairs and he imagined that the man was the one who had dispatched Whitely a few moments earlier. When Lionel came back to Grosvenor Square and reported what he had found out I paid him some more to be quiet about it and Amethyst stayed safe. The constabulary never made an arrest for the crime, but I did not want our family pulled through a long and gruelling investigation. Whitely had damaged us enough already.'

Daniel could not believe what he was hearing. 'Does anyone else know of this?'

'Black John Lionel, of course, but other than him, no one save the fellow who killed Whitely, I suppose, but he would hardly be speaking. I can tell you, though, that I hold absolutely no regrets for keeping quiet…'

'Good. I'd have done the same.'

'You would?'

He nodded. 'Without compunction, though I'd have probably shot him myself.'

Robert smiled, but sadness marked his eyes. 'Amy thinks it was the men from the docklands demanding money who tampered with the carriage. I let her believe that because it was easier than the truth and I even encouraged it. From the moment she found out Whitely was dead she began to live again. She knows nothing at all about my involvement with Black John Lionel and I sincerely hope that she never will. I haven't many months to live, so if you could find it in yourself to put my shocking confession aside until then I would be most grateful.'

Pouring out a large brandy, Daniel saw Robert's hand was shaking as he took it. 'In life there are things that have to be done.'

'Thank you.' The older man smiled, relief making him talk. 'It was my fault Amy ever met Whitely right from the beginning when he came to me as a clerk. At first he lived up to the promise of being meticulous and scrupulous, but it was not long before I began to think things were not as they should have been. His work began to suffer and then he made it his business to court Amethyst with all the stealth of a man who could see the acquisition of an easy fortune. There was no love in him, but he was clever in his concealing of it. When I understood that this was going to lead exactly where I didn't want it to go I offered him passage to the Americas and money to set up there as long as he never came within a hundred miles of us again. He married my daughter a week later. A week after that he stole the first thousand pounds and began his schemes to fleece the gentlemen of the *ton* out of their hard-earned cash.'

'Did Amethyst know what he was doing?'

'She was clever enough to recognise that the books were not adding up and that his "work" was dragging money out of our accounts. She got sadder daily and more removed from living and he had made it his mission by then to make certain she knew what he thought of her.'

'She didn't fight back?'

He shook his head. 'He was blackmailing me at that time and he had reason. I'd unwittingly taken up a contract that was a suspect cargo and it turned out to be stolen goods. On hindsight I think he also used the information to keep Amethyst biddable and she was trying to protect my reputation by remaining so. That is the worst of it.'

'My God. The bastard deserved a far slower death than the one he got, but after tonight we forget it. Move on and live.'

'I agree. There is one thing I would like to ask of you, though. In the light of what I have told you, would you be averse to me buying land in the area? I have seen a house not too far from here that I like the look of, though of course I would understand it if you felt uncertain about my presence here.'

'I have no reservations whatsoever and I know Amethyst will be pleased with the news.'

If Robert lived in Barnet, then Amethyst would want to stay at Montcliffe. To be back here for good was something Daniel had not expected, but the thought of his children here and their children marching down through the ages made a wonderful sense. He knew this place, these hills, the sound of the land and the timings of the seasons. He understood the cottars and the farm cycles and the birdsong and the plants in the wood. He had run free here for years of his life with his brother beside him and he had loved it. The realisation that Montcliffe Manor had always been in his blood whether he had known it or not gave him a new sense of belonging.

The man opposite was also a part of that. A friend, a confidant, a father who had taken the brave step of protecting his daughter in the only way he knew how.

'Before we left London, Robert, I had it put around in the docklands that I would not countenance any more attacks on Cameron personage or property. I have employed a couple of old soldiers that I trust to make certain that those who assaulted you near Hyde Park Corner will never threaten you again.'

'Then that has ended, too, and all we have now are new beginnings.' The lines of worry on Robert's face looked softer. 'I think my Susannah must be looking down on me to have made all this possible. Amethyst is very like her, you know. Loyal and fierce. Julia is the same.'

Lifting his glass of brandy Daniel offered up a toast. 'To our women then. May they long keep us safe.'

Her husband knocked at the door that was shared between the rooms as she sat at the dressing table in her night rail, brushing out the short length of her curls. Pulling on a wrap, she moved to turn the key placed on her side of the lock. When the portal opened Daniel stood dressed down in his breeches and an open shirt. He wore no cravat at all.

'Could we talk, Amethyst? In my chamber?'

'Of course.' She noticed he reached for the key and transferred it to his side of the door as they passed through.

The four-poster bed wrapped in dark brocade drew her eyes in a way it had not done earlier and she looked away quickly.

'Would you like a glass of wine?'

'I am not sure...'

'Just a little one? For bravery.'

The word brought a smile to her lips. 'Are you implying I might need it, my lord.'

He moved forward and took her hand in his own. 'Undoubtedly. But then, so will I, my lady, and in equal measure.'

Tonight he seemed different, lighter, less intimidating.

'I am starting to remember more from when I was sick.' He looked at her directly now, the green in his eyes full of question. 'And I am beginning to understand the meaning of some of the things you told me.'

I love you.

She had shouted it at him more than once when she had thought he might not live.

'I remember you saying something about for ever as you urged me to fight. Without you I might have given up and let the darkness claim me, but you shook me awake and gave me your words. So now my question is this: is our marriage only one of convenience, Amethyst, or could we find more within it?'

Not the proclamation she had hoped for and dressed in a lacy nightgown with a large bed a few feet away the language of lust must be taken into account. How much more did he want from her? She swallowed. With only a mention of love she would allow him everything.

'More?'

'Between us,' he answered. 'Like this.'

His fingers crept to the ties of her wrap and as he undid the ribbons she felt the swish of satin pool about her feet in a single and quiet sigh. Now she only wore her thin and sheer silk-and-lace nightgown, sleeveless and cut low, the lace hiding nothing. She made herself stand still, in the warmth of his room and under his gaze.

'You are the most beautiful woman I have

ever seen, sweetheart.' One finger traced the outline of her right breast and stopped at the nipple. She took in a breath and waited, the thick ache of her want almost a physical thing.

The magic in his touch and words was like tinder to dry kindling. Fire flame, with the burn of a need that consumed her. Her, Amethyst Amelia with her failed first marriage and her ugly port-wine birthmark. Her, the daughter of trade and of commerce, an unchosen bride who had instigated a marriage of convenience with an aristocrat that had left him no other choice but to sign.

Yet he still thought her beautiful.

'I love you.' She could no longer find it in herself to pretend or to be cautious. 'I love you with all of my heart, Daniel.'

His smile came quickly. 'Ahhh, my Amethyst. I dreamed you had said it and now I know.'

His thumb began to move across her nipple and she could not stop the arching want or her shaky breath or the way her hand fell on top of his, keeping him there at his ministrations, urging response. She could not stop the surge of joy either that swept away sense and left her reeling. For him. For her husband. For a lord who had set her free.

Tears rolled down her cheeks.

'Love me, back,' she whispered.

'I do,' he returned and, lifting her into his arms, took her to his bed.

He laid her down carefully, the long lines of her legs against his counterpane, the fairness of her skin and the heavy bounty of her breasts.

Waiting.

And then it hit him, hard in the place about his heart, that she was his. His bride. His for ever. And she loved him. Another thought came at about the same time as that one. The chaos of her first marriage with Whitely pointed to a lack of true intimacy. Would she allow him all that he wanted or would she be fearful?

Her hand came across his and he could feel the shaking. 'Whitely never...' She did not finish.

'Bedded you?' He suddenly knew that was what she was saying to him, the shocking truth of it immediate as he recalled Lucien telling him of Whitely's groin accident as a child.

'I think he was...incapable.'

'He has not touched you as a husband?'

The curls shook as she moved her head slowly.

Relief flooded in, but he had never lain with an innocent before and the blood that pounded was not conducive to the patience he would need. No, not at all. His rod was stiff straight as he wiped his hair back and took a breath.

She must have seen his consternation, for she began to speak again. 'But I have seen the animals at the farm at Dunstan House and we have always kept horses, so I know the way of mating and all that it includes.'

'Are you trying to reassure me?' He couldn't strip the amazement from his words. Could she think him untutored in the art of lovemaking?

'I will be twenty-seven next February, and so I am hardly a girl, but if it is reassurance you need…'

He stopped her by leaning forward and laying his mouth against her own, hard and unyielding by way of reply. The lemon scent of her so familiar and her curls were short in his hands. Unlike any other woman, strong and honest and his.

Slanting his kiss, he brought her in closer, his breath ragged, his want untrammelled and the need for possession desperate.

'I do not think you quite understand how it

is, my love,' he said softly when he raised his head and looked at her. 'But I promise that you soon will.'

She felt his other hand lift away the thin-and-nothing barrier of her lacy gown. Naked. Exposed. His eyes met hers before wandering into places no one else had ever seen.

And then he knelt and brought his mouth to the mark at her thigh, the wet warmth of his tongue tracing her shame as if it was beautiful, too; as if the redness was indeed the kiss of the fairies of which her mother had spoken. No quick exploration, either, but a generous lengthy loving that took away all worry and replaced it with only hope.

But other things were happening, his hand against her thigh, the throb inside her between her legs, the longing for a touch she had no notion of, there at the centre of her being.

He stood and doffed his shirt and the brown hardness of him took her breath away.

'I want you, Amethyst.'

'Why?' The word was whispered, brave against the gaze of pale green.

'Because I love you.' Simple. Quiet. He did not drop his glance or qualify the truth with other lesser things and her heart swelled with joy.

His trousers were unbuttoned and his boots untied and then he was naked, too, the candlelight in the room flickering over them both, sculpting contours in flame. Dark against light, hard against soft. His body held masculine grace tempered with the scars of battles that had long since been fought. Touching a knotted line on the sharp bone of his hip, she traced it down.

Then his mouth came across hers. Skin against skin and bone against bone. She caught a dark desire inside him as his tongue tasted, the strength and the fear.

'I should not wish to hurt you.' Whispered close through breath and heartbeat.

'You won't.'

The tension in him was coiled like a spring, the soldier who had always taken action now stymied by something he had not expected. ''Tis a first for me as well, this.'

She only smiled.

'I haven't been a saint, but I have not deflowered a woman before either.'

Deflowered? God, he was making a hash of this, talking like a schoolboy in the moments he should have just shut up and got on with it.

But there was something in the gentleness of her gift and words that made him…nervous.

This was the first time she had lain with a man and from all he had ever heard women needed it to be special.

Special when all he could think about was pushing deep inside of her and claiming her in that one momentous final moment of elation that made a man weep with the beauty of it.

The velvet-brown in her eyes was soft, understanding, almost gold under the candlelight.

'Love me, Daniel.'

'For ever, my love.'

And then it was simple, the tight lines of their bodies together, his hand cupping her bottom and bringing her over the hard rod of his need. An opening slick with wetness and a quiet push within.

He heard her gasp and stopped, slowly, slowly, but for ever onwards until the hilt of him was buried in the warmth of her flesh and against the edge of her womb.

'Mine.' He said the word in wonder and watched her take it in, saw the flickering pain on her face change into surprise and then into fire. Felt the waves of her own ecstasy against him, claiming and clenching until he could not know where he ended and Amethyst began, the melded aching orgasm taking them both above thought and reason to a place where nothing existed, save for them.

Suspended there. Without time. Without surroundings. Clinging to desire until the very last tiny echoes had subsided and the world crashed once again into reality.

'Thank you.' He could not remember ever saying that to a woman after making love, but all he could feel was gratitude, his seed holding them together and the hollow beat of his heart finally quieting.

Usually he got up straight away, the feeling of intimacy threatening somehow and empty. But here, now, his hand fell against her back and he held her close, her warmth of skin and her legs straddling his.

More. He wanted her again. Wanted to slip in and stay there for ever. His member rose and nudged her thigh and she simply opened her legs and let him enter.

This time it was slower, the slickness allowing an easy entrance, the rise and fall of her breasts against his hands as he took her. His tempo quickened just with the thought.

* * *

She was rushing again to that place she had had no notion of, the high breathless plane of wanton relief. She could feel herself reaching, tipping into him, his shaft within her deep.

She heard herself cry out, guttural and primal, noises that she had never thought to make before, sounds from the very soul of her need.

Again. And again. Boneless and formless. And this time when the final pulses came she dug her nails into his skin and marked him with the loving, long runnels of redness against the brown.

Afterwards she could not move, but lay there across him, still joined, still feeling the heaviness of him within her, and then she slept.

Birdsong woke him, the twelve-hour candles burned towards the end of their usefulness, the drips of wax across the holders opaquely white and twisted.

Daniel breathed out and watched the last of the night turn into dawn, streaked with the pink of a new day. The sounds of the house were quiet. The swish of an early maid's skirts as she walked the passageway, the creak of timber shedding off the cold of night, the creeping plant outside his window, its greened tendrils knocking against the glass.

All the sounds he had heard for all of the years of his life. And now there was a new one. Amethyst's quiet breathing, her eyelashes long against her cheeks.

His bride. His wife. His lover now, her body claimed as his own.

Would there be a child? Would this night bring the fruit of conception and the promise of another generation of Wyldes born into the lineage of Montcliffe?

If it was a boy, they could call him Nigel and this time he would get it right. If it was a girl, he hoped that they might find a name of a gemstone as Robert and Susannah had and then he could also call his daughter 'my jewel'.

'What are you thinking?' Amethyst's voice was soft with the morning.

'Of you and of us and our future. I'd like children…'

She pushed herself up at that and her hand went beneath the covers, across his chest and then his stomach to the budding hardness of his flesh.

'So would I.'

'Now?' He could see in her face the languid hope of sex.

Turning over, he brought her beneath him, covering her smallness with his body and finding the very centre of her with his fingers before once again entering in.

When she awoke next he was not there, the day without showing a full sun and a cloudless sky.

Her eyes went to the clock on the mantel. Almost one o'clock. Looking around, she saw piles of books and an old piano she had not noticed yesterday. A globe and guns stacked on small shelves completed the tableau beside it.

A man's room, nothing feminine within it, save for her tangled in the sheets and naked, her thighs tight with his seed and her nipples tender from his kissing.

Like a child she had held him there, his hair dark against the white of her skin. Her hand fell across her thigh and inwards, the throb of delight still present under a different ache. She smiled. Not like the animals in the barnyard after all. The slight tip of her hips brought the feeling back and she reached for a momentary echo, pushing down on the bone of her groin, guided by some ancient knowledge.

Daniel Wylde had healed her and made her whole. He had taken all the doubts and turned them into certainty; the sureness of being loved and of loving back as well.

A gift of place and of beauty, the heart and body and soul kind of love her parents had known and of which the great stories told.

Her story now. No longer blinded by shame. Her fingers traced the mark on her thigh and she remembered his mouth there. Not ugly. Not unsightly.

But beautiful.

He had called her that so many times over so many hours and in the sunshine of a new day she finally felt it.

She came downstairs much later, having bathed and washed her hair and tidied up the scramble of sheets upon the master bed. She felt different, the soreness in her private places only adding to the illusion. She felt wanton too, her mind going to the hours between now and when they could again be in each other, feeling the heat of their loving.

Only the Earl was in attendance at the table.

'Your father and Julia have been journeying around the countryside all day and have sent word that they will be down in an hour or so. Perhaps we might look over the garden before we eat as it will be a while before it is served.

Hope soared. 'I would like that.'

Outside the courtyard was empty. Leading her around a corner under the overhang of stone, he found a position that shielded them from any unsuspecting servant who might be walking the paths.

He was kissing her before she even turned, hard desperate kisses that spoke of all the frenzy she herself felt, and when they came up for breath he held her closely against him.

'Will there ever be a time when I see you without wanting you?'

She laughed. 'I hope not.' Her finger traced the line of his lips.

'If you keep doing that we won't be having any dinner.' The smile in his words was as obvious as the need in his eyes. 'Would you like to see how Deimos is faring? John has been asking after you, too. I think you have earned his respect as a healer, Amethyst, which, believe me, is a hard thing to do.'

'He has been here at Montcliffe for a long time, then?' she asked him as they walked.

'Since I was a boy. It was John who taught me a lot of the tricks of the trade. His own father was the stablemaster at Montcliffe before him and his father's father before that.'

'History,' she said quietly. 'That is what I love about this place. I have never been so much a part of what has come before.'

'Or after,' he said and brought her fingers to his lips. 'I'd like lots of children to see Montcliffe prosper.'

'Then let us try again for the first after dinner,' she whispered and laughed as he turned towards the stables.

Her father and Julia were both waiting in the small salon next to the dining room when they returned and it seemed to Amethyst that her world had rolled over into something different. Papa looked the happiest she had ever seen him and her own heart sang with the promise of life. The doctor had been right after all: hope was the best medicine for any ailment. She knew he was not cured, but he was definitely happy.

'We have some wonderful news to give you—' Robert's voice was light '—and I have had wine sent up from London to celebrate it with.' He gestured to the bottles in front of him with the four fluted glasses standing beside them. 'Julia has done me the honour of agreeing to become my wife and I have signed the deeds today on a house not far from here in which we intend to live.'

'I hope you will give us your blessing, Amethyst? I realise it might seem a sudden thing, but sometimes one just knows.' Julia's voice was soft. 'I swear I shall make it my goal in life to keep your father healthy.'

Sometimes one just knows.

Reaching for Daniel's hand, Amethyst understood exactly what Julia was referring to as his fingers tightened about her own.

'I would be delighted to welcome you to the family, Julia, as I haven't seen Papa smile so much in years.'

As the wine was poured Robert handed them all a glass. 'I would like to make a toast, then, to for ever. For us all.'

Much later they lay together in the main chamber, the time well after one in the morning.

'I love you more than life itself, my Amethyst,' Daniel said into the darkness and the sound of it curled into his heart. 'And I am glad that you waited for me.'

She smiled. 'Gerald finally did me a favour.' Her words were soft against his chest. 'If he had been a better man, I might not have met you.'

'He is dead. He will never hurt us again.'

'And the others. The ones who tampered with our carriage on the road to Leicester?'

'They will not harm us either, I promise.' He tried to keep the anger from the edge of his words.

'Papa was right to choose you as our saviour. He would not have managed to scare them away all by himself.'

'Your father is an amazing man. I think he would do almost anything for love and he's a lot stronger than he looks.'

'Perhaps with Julia's care he can confound all the doctors, though there will come a day when…' She did not go on.

'If we have a boy first, let's name him Robert.' Nigel could wait, Daniel thought, but for Amethyst's father time was fading and the sheer bravery of the older man had never ceased to amaze him. He hoped he could be half the father to his own children as the old timber merchant had been to Amethyst.

'Perhaps when Gwen comes to visit us we might have my grandfather here as well. A change in scenery would do him good and a time away from my mother might be just the thing he needs,' he suggested.

'I'd like that. We could take him to visit my father and show him the horses and…'

She stopped talking when he kissed her.

He had no wish at all to return to society, but resolved to make his life here, amongst the green hills and valleys of Montcliffe. Tracing a pattern across the freckles on his wife's shoulders, Daniel began to tell her of Nigel.

The last secrets were almost the hardest, but he had to let her know of the man his brother had been and of the death that he had chosen.

'He left a note for me with my grandfather and it was not at all what I was expecting. I think he was depressed.'

The night closed about them as he spoke and the shame of suicide lessened under her quiet and gentle acceptance.

Epilogue

Daniel sat with Robert and Lucien in the small sitting chamber off the main bedroom, his eyes glancing at the clock every few minutes.

'We should have gone to London for the birth.' He had told Amethyst this again and again, but she would not listen. Standing, he walked to the window and looked outside.

Oh, God, please let my wife and child be safe.

The refrain had been his mantra for weeks and weeks, words that rolled around in his mind first thing in the morning and last thing at night. He had tried to keep his fear from showing, but he had been sleeping badly for months now and the dreams he did have, if he was lucky to slumber, seemed to mirror his every anxiety. If anything happened to Amethyst, he would want to be dead too. If she died, then he would want to follow, in his heart and his soul and his body

'Susannah used to say that giving birth was a woman's glory and her triumph for being feminine.'

At this moment Robert's sentiments were the last things Daniel wanted to hear. Glory. Triumph. There were so many other words more apt to use as the cries of his labouring wife had fallen down into whimpers.

This was when they died. When their energy was spent and their blood was thin and the will to live waned under constant pain. God, how much practice had he had in that on the battlefields?

But he was a man and strong and fit while she…

A single shout had him at the door before anyone could stop him and he was through into the master chamber, ignoring the protests of Julia, Christine Howard and the midwife.

Amethyst's forehead was slick with sweat when he reached her and the red blush of blood on the sheets beneath was telling.

'Dr MacKenzie will be here soon, my love.'

She gripped his hand.

'I cannot do this without you, Daniel. Please, I want you here…'

He looked around the room, the pale face of Julia and the flushed one of Christine. Only the midwife looked unconcerned.

The midwife had all the herbs and candles his wife had instructed her to bring, but still it did not seem to be enough. Fear rushed in like the enemy and he made himself breathe through it.

For so many battles and for so many years he had found in himself the strength to forsake dread and fight, yet in the end this was the most important battle of them all.

He turned to his wife and smiled, hoping that the glory and triumph of which Robert had spoken just a few moments past was there on his face to see.

'This baby needs to come, my darling, and together we can help it arrive.'

Her fingers entwined around his own and she nodded. 'It won't be long,' she said quietly and then stiffened, her hand squeezing his in a grip that was surprising.

An hour and a half later Amethyst sat changed and washed, her hair arranged in two short thick plaits by Christine, and the swaddled baby at her breast.

'You did it, Amethyst,' Lucien's sister gushed. 'Sapphire is the most beautiful child I have ever seen.'

With a fuzz of blonde covering her head and pale brown eyes Daniel could not help but agree. Her grandfather had his own way of showing relief as he wiped the tears from his eyes.

'Sapphire Susannah Wylde. Your mother would have been pleased.' Robert's voice quivered with the poignancy of memory.

Lucien stood back from the frivolity, the birthing room and a small baby well out of his realm of comfort, but he took a box from his pocket and presented it to Amethyst.

'This comes from my own estate. A moonstone for June and new beginnings. Appropriate, I think.'

The bracelet was entwined in white gold and pearls, an expensive treasure that Daniel knew Lucien could ill afford to give, but his wife's smile when she saw it was priceless.

'Sapphire's second piece of jewellery,' she said and held the gemstone up to the light, 'for Daniel found a tiny bejewelled cap this morning amongst the Montcliffe treasures.' The crystalline structures within the moonstone made it shimmer with every shade of the rainbow, prisms of light filling the room.

And for Daniel the moonstone was exactly what his life now reminded him of. Full, joyous, colourful and rich.

Rich in people and in structure, and in laughter and memories. Rich in place and belonging and happiness. The true riches, he thought, are the ones never imagined.

When Amethyst took his hand in her own he looked down and smiled.

He was home, at last, and at peace with his two most precious jewels. Home in the belonging of family.

* * * * *